Colin Rae Brown

Noble love and other poems

Colin Rae Brown

Noble love and other poems

ISBN/EAN: 9783337206673

Printed in Europe, USA, Canada, Australia, Japan

Cover: Foto ©Andreas Hilbeck / pixelio.de

More available books at **www.hansebooks.com**

Noble Love.

NOBLE LOVE

AND

OTHER POEMS

BY

COLIN RAE-BROWN.

W. H. HODGE AND CO., PRINTERS, RATHBONE PLACE, W.

NOBLE LOVE,

AS

EXEMPLIFYING A PHASE

OF

ENGLISH CHARITY

IS

RESPECTFULLY DEDICATED

TO THE

BARONESS BURDETT COUTTS.

CONTENTS.

OUTLINES IN VERSE.

Contents.

PROEM.

READ not the lowliness of thy estate,
For ev'ry eager, earnest-purposed soul
There is a highway to nobility.
First know thyself, and then an orbit choose
Where thou canst move and shine—diffusing light,
Yet being its recipient evermore.

Above, beneath, around us—and within
Our own mysterious beings—Knowledge dwells.
Nor are the most exalted heights of fame
Denied to him whose accident of birth
Precludes the hope of adventitious aid.
Brave leaders in the forward march of mind—
In purpose strong—have from the ranks upris'n.
Onward and upward toiling, undismayed,
Until the goal was gained, the guerdon won.
What though we heir not titles, or broad lands?

B

The glorious empires of recorded thought—
The boundless worlds of mind—are all our own :
By these enriched, no man need think him poor,
Or murmur at the meanness of his birth :
Ennobled by their wealth, the peasant may
To intellectual monarchy aspire,
And win and wear its crown right regally!

Had Burns lived only for his humble plough,
Content to master matter and observe
The varied aspects of successive crops,
How much the poorer must the world have been—
Nor threw he off the yoke of honest toil
While summering amongst the flowers of song,
But plodded ever on in Labour's track
Through all the changing seasons and the years.

Untutored minds bewail the lack of time,
And sigh for leisure and reflective ease ;
But they who walk betimes in wisdom's paths,
And pile her treasures up for future days,
Are never destitute of inward joys.
Thus heavenward souls communion ever have
With things immortal, while the outward man,

In business diligent—improving time—
But spins or weaves, or hews the sturdy oak ;
Or sows, or reaps, or drives his team afield ;
Or quarries strata after strata up ;
Or buys or sells, or builds or breaketh down ;
Or guides his rapid pen through ledger-lore ;
Or steers his vessel 'midst the howling storm ;
Or leads his army on, like Havelock.
Such lives are jewels in the crown of God,
And through Eternity shall sparkle there—
No limit to the setting of that crown,
No soul so lowly that it may not rise
And add a glory to His diadem !

NOBLE LOVE.

BOOK FIRST.

EVANDER was a child of charity,
    An orphan even from his earliest years—
And owning nothing but the honoured name
And brave achievements of a humble sire,
Bequeathed ere yet his tongue that name could lisp ;
While, all too soon for her dear babe's good thrift,
The widow'd mother, pining, droopt and died.
A British sailor of the noblest stamp,
Evander's father at his post expired.
His lion heart, without a tremor, felt
The life-blood oozing from a deadly wound—
Tiller in hand, the word was, " Hard-a-port,"
He ran the braggart foe-ship bravely down,
Breathed his last prayer, and died a hero's death !
We bless thee, England, for thy Charities,

Dispensing blessings great as manifold,

Ever distilling Mercy's precious dews

In fruitful showers with healing virtues fraught :

In one of these Evander found a home

And, 'midst its comforts, soon unlearn'd his loss.

Blest with a kindly matron's sympathy—

Her fond endearments gaining rich reward

In his young heart's outwelling gratitude-

The boy grew up contented with his lot :

God bless thy charities, dear Native Land !

God bless the Givers ! bless them, one and all !

Friends ever are inestimable gifts,

And worthy of our dearest love—our constant care :

Life wanting such becomes a joyless round

Yielding no smiles in joy, no tears in grief—

O bind them strongly with the cords of love !

Forgive the hasty word, forget the fault

Which they, ingenuous, seek not to conceal.

To what shall we compare Sincerity—

A sun whose bright effulgence never sets—

A star whose lustre fades not with the dawn —

A bow of peace that never disappears :

A bright green spot on Care's wide sterile waste
A shelt'ring tree whose leafage never fails
A well of living waters, deep and cool ;
A helper o'er Life's hard and stony paths :
A trusty pilot through Time's stormy seas -
A faithful chart, and compass ever true—
A beacon set amidst the shoals and reefs—
A safe, unshifting, pleasant anchorage :
A rock whose firm foundations never shake :
A watchful sentinel that never sleeps—
A weapon to defend, not to defy :
A clasping hand that never grows relaxt
A breast that never harbours cold deceit -
A voice whose utterance is ever true :
A home to which the trusting heart repairs
When cold Adversity hath winnow'd friends
Life's never failing, ever true delight—?

The gentle boy became an ardent youth
And forth adventured on the world's wide way :
Begirt with principles of sternest mould
He strove but to excel where virtue led,
So grew in favour and advancement met.
Oft granted leisure, as a re-reward.

He roamed afar through intellectual climes
And culled the fairest flowers that in them grew.
Though in luxuriance, as in grace and strength,
His young imagination revelled free,
He had betimes been taught, and ever strove,
To prune and train its rich fertility—
Thus, like a goodly plant, in kindly soil,
Well cared for ev'ry day, it throve apace.

External Nature, and the God it preacht,
A fervent worshipper in him had found—
At morn, at noon, at twilight's pensive hour,
Or when the dark of contemplative Night
Revealed Creation's vast magnificence.
He never sighed for Autumn's falling leaves,
Or grieved when Winter sealed fruition up,
But saw in ev'ry change a law fulfilled :
He dearly loved the young and bright-eyed Spring
That jewels earth with buds and promise flowers,
Jonquil and crocus, snowdrop and blue bell.

How fresh, how gay, how beautiful is Spring !
How pleasant to the sight its opening charms,
How welcome its exhilarating air,

How sweet the joyous carol of its birds!
The quicken'd grain shoots through the yielding soil,
Its tomb that was, its smiling birthplace now,
Re-robing Earth with tender greenery:
All nature lives again to gladden Man—
Breathing to Heaven an incense-laden hymn—
O that his heart, renewed, could so rejoice,
And, with pure off'rings, glad his inner world!

Thou art all bright and beautiful, sweet Spring!
Thy silv'ry streamlets, dancing down the hills,
Leap joyously into the glens deep pools,
And thence emerge—in silent, shining forms
That wend their way to fill pellucid lakes,
Whence flow the rivers on their seaward way.
The young year's sun is prodigal of light—
Arrayed at early morn in brilliant state,
He scattereth sublime irradiance
And with transcendant glory floods the world:
New life and being calling into play,
The mountain and the valley he makes glad—
Benignantly revivifying all.
Season of Hope, be gracious unto us,
Revive our bodies, and our souls relume,

And be true herald of a coming time
When Error shall forsake God's noblest work,
And disenthrallèd mind have sov'reign sway!

Evander loved the promise-laden Spring,
But he adored the Summer's golden prime,
And oft hath told how, at the early dawn,
He sought the summit of a fav'rite cliff
And watched the Morn put forth her lovely arms—
To draw apart the filmy folds of cloud
That screened her virgin couch: she, smiling thence,
As joy-expectant as a fair young bride
Whose love's blest consummation is at hand.
Beneath him lay the sea, waveless and still,
Stretching far out—away, and yet away—
A vast expanse that kissed the distant sky.
At times, a whisp'ring breeze passed o'er his head
And down the cliffs, saluting on its way
The lone sea-flower, and shaking off the dew;
Or, floating o'er the sea, blew ripples up,
That danced with glee as rose the King of Day—
Who spent his hours dispensing wreathèd smiles,
Then sank to rest in mellow radiance robed:
An amber, deep'ning to a crimson glow,

That with rich splendours canopied his bed,
And shed a burning glory o'er the deep!

Sweet Summer is the year's bright honeymoon,
And never bridegroom longed more ardently
Than did Evander for the blooming May—
In votive lay, thus fashioned, hailing her approach—
"Come, gentle Summer, woo us with thy smiles,
Unfold thy blossomed wings, and swiftly come!
O tarry not, sweet season of the year,
With plenty come to crown the blesséd Spring!
Pour forth, in floods, thy gushing melodies,
Make every grove a paradise of song,
And breathe upon us, in soft sighing gales,
Delicious odours from the opening flowers!"

The forest, and the humbler woods and groves,
Affording kindly and refreshing shade,
Oft drew him to their most secluded nooks,
And dear to him the meadows and the fields—
O ye are very pleasant, ye green fields!
Ye are so soft, so bright and beautiful,
So welcome and refreshing to the eyes
Long prisoned in the unromantic town!

True, a divinity reigns everywhere,

Deep in the dark and disembowell'd earth,

Or on the giant mountain's dizziest peak,

But O, ye dwellers by the wood and fields

Who are not lacerated by the sights

That in the city wound and rend the heart,

Praise God continually for your estate—

So fraught wtth the primæval bliss of man !

NOBLE LOVE.

BOOK SECOND.

SUCH were the joys Evander's manhood knew,
But all his boyhood years were closely pent
Within the busy city's stony bounds;
And wheresoe'er he went, or what befell,
World-wonder London never was forgot.
Far, far away, his memory oft recalled
Those narrow, winding streets, and tortuous lanes,
O'er which St. Paul's in solemn grandeur looms.

Immensity of cities! dense as vast!
A Babel and a Babylon in one!
Colossus-like, astride the noble Thames,
With feet on either side, thy gods are seen—
Thy Gog and Magog, venerably great.
What crowded hives of bustling human life

In thee—gregarious—swarm, and buzz, and hum.

Throng upon throng, a nation in themselves—

Earth's grandest type of Cosmopolitism !

What lights and shadows on thy surface play.

Constant in nothing save their constant change—

What hopes and fears in thy big heart contend,

Joys multitudinous and countless woes—

What startling revelations would appear

In one brief day's eventful history—

What dark. unfathomed, tearful tragedies—

What bright beatitudes of Peace and Love !

Virtue and Vice, commingling. yet apart.

Pass and repass thy crowded thoroughfares

From hour to hour, in motley multitudes—

Motley in purpose as in garb and form :

Each, with a separate mission to fulfil,

Must for himself go quarry out a path

Through which, instinctively, he makes his way-

Alike unheeded and unheedingly.

The Sins and Sorrows of the Cities thrive,

Till want. and woe, and misery, and crime,

Have ceased to wake our horror. or surprise.

But are with stolid glances met and passed
Familiar institutions of the age.

Almighty God, our Father, and our Friend,
Who to the freedom of his will hath left.
In Thine own image formed, the creature, Man,
How must Thy universal ear be filled
With plaints and sobs by mortal ears unheard
Thy universal eye, with sadd'ning sights
Unpitied and unseen by all but Thee!
Behind the Veil, unknown to mortal ken,
There lies a world of dread Realities
Vast regions, all unknown and unexplored
Dark vales of Sorrow which no strangers tread,
Great seas of Grief unploughed by foreign keels:
Behind the Veil, unknown, unheard, unseen,
By all save Thee, more dramas are enact
Than on the open stage of daily life.

Dahomey's bloody rites appal the mind
And Nature shudders at their dark details,
Yet here, in this most honoured Christian land,
This vaunted cradle of the goodly great,
Religion's model home and Freedom's boast,
Our darker horrors make the angels weep.

Behind the Veil, with poison, cord, or knife,

Infanticide pursues its hideous course ;

At times, in trembling, hesitating mood,

But oft'ner with a firm, relentless will

That knows no pity, anguish, or remorse.

Could we but see the shambles where each babe

Awaits, perhaps in sleep, its coming doom,

Or watch the ruthless hand that crushes out

The life so lately given, or hear the voice

Whose tender bleatings fail to touch the heart !

Alas ! we do not wish to fret our lives,

Or care to know what lies behind the Veil,

With more than ostrich-ignorance to blame—

With cruel crime, most foul and pitiless,

Red-reeking in our midst, our very homes,

We only waste the time in vain regrets

And nurse the hideous Evil we deplore !

" Sham " is on many a lofty forehead writ—

Could we but pierce that flimsy cuticle

And read the fest'ring characters beneath

The unctuous polish of the shining brow—

The seeming not the real doth obtain,

The counterfeit more current is than gold,

And forged humanity may pass with ease.
Would we were gifted with unerring skill
To separate the sterling from the base—
To ratify the same with honest seal,
Whose lasting impress should instruct the world !
O were it meet for us to travel through
The Vast array of Insincerity
With which the Age is heavily surcharged—
So glossed with smooth Hypocrisy,
So hideous and revolting to the eye
Which through no false, expedient medium sees—
We would but find Experience sadder grow,
And quite one half the world existing as
If Earth-probation and the Life to come
Were mere inventions, or deluding Shams !

Evander was a frequent, welcome guest
At his kind master's hospitable home,
And ever as the Day of Rest wore round,
He bent his footsteps thitherward at morn.
The Grange was centred in a fair domain
Remote from prying eyes, and guarded by
A noble army of gigantic trees
Whose gnarled and twisted trunks, grown hoar with age,

Were netted round with hardy parasites.

The house, a treasure to artistic eyes,

Was roofed with strangely convoluted tiles,

Each hollow filled with debris of dead leaves—

A richly blended mass of red and green—

That had to dust returned, and then giv'n birth

To strips of velvet turf, begemmed and starred

With flowers that from wind-wafted seeds had sprung :

Rich clust'ring ivy, thick and glossy leafed,

The pointed gables graced, and, clambering o'er

The high-peaked windows, round them hung

In fluttering festoons that swept the porch—

Which, frail with age, and winter's scathing storms,

Was scarcely fit to bear its scented thatch

Of jasmine, interwove with passion-flower ;

Yet none might dare remove it from the spot

Where, many years before, it had been reared

By one who fought his country's battles well,

And in her annals lives a deathless life.

The quality in heroes that befits

Them most for greatness is Sincerity,

And he might well have been its archætype.

On Truth's foundation moral grandeur rests,

And Herbert's sire embraced it from his youth,
And lived and died an honourable man.
Like rectitude of purpose swayed his son,
Whose simple word was known to be his bond.
His was that consciousness of worth, and wealth,
Which moves along with firm, elastic step,
With look serene, and fearless, open brow.
Keel after keel of his ploughed foreign Seas,
And where the Ganges rolls its mighty tide
The name was potent as at home on Change.

The faithful servant must needs fervent be,
And only in an atmosphere of love
Can fervour thrive and bear its goodly fruit :
No law but that of Kindness safely binds—
Its welcome chains defy Misfortune's stroke,
And are but strengthen'd by its heaviest blow.
Would that the world at large with Herbert thought,
Would that all strove, with acts like his, to win
Their hands and hearts whose lot is servitude !

One smiling Sabbath morn, in pleasant June,
Evander took his way towards the Grange,
Through still suburban lanes and winding paths

Dower'd with the honeysuckle's balmy breath,
And garlanded with modest wilding flowers
That know no culture save the sun and dew—
Arched here and there, o'erhead, with branching screens.
And thrid beneath by voiceless rivulets:
All nature seemed to court serene repose,
In silent worship, mutely eloquent.

Thrice blesséd day of holy calm and quiet,
Foreshadowing the Sabbath of the soul!
First fruit of the Redeemer's sacred blood
Shed for the sins of Men on Calvary!
They who by toil invade thy needed rest ,
Are very aliens to the Commonwealth,
And spoile·s of a glorious heritage!

Sweet Sabbath morn!—be welcome evermore!
Amidst the populous City's streams of life,
Where many hundred thousand human hearts
Beat high or low, or cease, as Time rolls on:
Where ev'ry bosom hath its freight of joy,
Or woe, to bear along life's changing sea—

Upon the mountain tops, where silence reigns

Supreme o'er all, as at Creation's birth ;
Or where th' unlorded winds can rage at will,
Careering madly through the mist and cloud—

In caves or glens where, in the olden time,
Protesting fa·hers worshipt, battle clad,
And praised the God they loved, with sword in hand—

On the gay meadow, in the shady dell,
Enamell'd with bright clusters of sweet flowers,
Wild flowers, that bloom alike for rich and poor,
And freely gift their od'rous sweets to all—

In grey Cathedrals, monuments of Art,
When Art was rich in its primeval wealth ;
Or in the humble Village Sanctuary,
Where Praise ascendeth from untutored lips
And finds a welcome at the Throne of Grace :
Coequal with the more pretentious strains
That swell through fretted and re-echoing aisles
Resounding the sonorous organ's peals—

Among the tombstones, eloquently dumb,
Suggesting thoughts that overflow the heart-

As all the Lights and Shadows of the Past,
Strangely commingling with the Present, meet,
And quietly shadow forth what is to come—

Upon the stately vessel's spacious deck,
Walled round by landless space, and vaulted o'er
With fleecy clouds and sky of azure hue,
While gently swelling waves her sides caress,
Or curl and foam around the bounding prow—

At the far prairie's verge, a vast expanse,
Beneath the shadows of centurial trees,
Where wand'rers from our native land encamp
To keep the Sabbath as a Day of Rest—

Sweet Sabbath Day!—the same on land or sea.
If but the heart be faithful to its Lord—
Long may thy blessings glad this world of ours !
Increasing as they flow, till Sin and Death
Are crusht beneath His Feet—who yet shall reign
As Prince of Peace, the blest Millenial King !

Such lofty thoughts Evander's mind engaged,
Though, with unwonted haste, he hurried on—

To meet that " Little Edith " he had heard
About so oft, Herbert's long absent child :
His steps were swift, his heart was light and free,
And, all exhilarant, he gained the Grange.

From early dawn, he had been quaffing up
Those sparkling wines of intellectual growth
That flow, matured, through old poetic lore,
And felt as joyous as the Bird of Morn
Who knows its wings are gifted with the power
To soar, or circle, wheresoe'er it will :
He, like the happy bee, knew where to find
The tempting sweets he loved and cherisht most,
So lived an easy and contented life—
From morn to eve, from year to year. the same.

NOBLE LOVE.

BOOK THIRD.

FATE lies beyond control—Evander found
The little Edith cast in fairest mould
Of womanhood, and, straightway, lost his heart.
The hot blood reddened o'er his cheek and brow,
And when he dared again to look,
A kindred blush the maiden's face o'erspread,
While downcast eyes spake volumes to his soul—
In short, they met, and loved—the old, old tale !

At Herbert's door a grievous error lay—
When but an infant prattling on the knee,
He had betrothed his daughter to the heir
Of goodly acres marching with his own :
As both domains had once his father's been,

He thought the joint entail thus fashioned forth
A vict'ry wrung from adverse circumstance,
And held its consummation dear as life :
This bond had been the grandsire's earnest prayer,
And when the old man's sand of life ran low
They set the seal to the betrothal deed—
That he might die content—so runs the tale.

Unconscious as the graceful bounding roe
Of coming battue, and the murd'rous ball,
The gentle Edith grew to womanhood
Withouten ken of this unholy pact.
So, with a full, free heart—as pure as free—
She laid the off'ring of her virgin love
Before that shrine of which Evander seemed
Presiding idol, and her soul's desire.

That same sweet Sabbath day, with like intent,
Eyes, other than Evander's, Edith's sought,
But failed to draw from her's that warm response
Which flasht love's golden sunshine o'er his heart—
Young Elmore sought her glance with ardent zeal,
And with her father plied a fluent tongue,
But ne'er a word of the betrothal bond,
And ne'er a look from the heart-captured maid.

So weeks wore on, while, Desdemona-like,
Edith had learnt Evander's simple tale—
And learnt it but to weave around his heart,
More firm and close, the tendrils of her own :
Blending their kindred beings into one,
Each for the other lived a new-born life
And in their present joy read future bliss.

He never loved before, or counted love
Necessity of his, but now it seemed
As if he could not live one little hour
Without its joy—enthralling heart and soul :
And, ev'ry day, he thanked and praised his God
For dow'ring him with such a precious gift,
And ever thus his inner voice would sing :
" I never loved before ! I never felt
Such high and holy aspirations fill
My breast and interpenetrate my heart—
Such yearnings to prove worthy of the love
Which so enriches and makes glad my soul :
My own beloved Edith ! now I feel
As if one half my being had gone forth
To dwell for ever in thy heart of hearts—
To be for ever near thee, night and day,

To guide and guard thee, present though unseen,
To whisper life-devotion in thine ear,
To press love's ardent kisses on thy lips,
To lock thee in affection's fond embrace—
To rest for ever on thy bosom's bliss ! "

He never loved before ! the world to him
Had been a desert, though he wist it not—
Now, on a smiling oasis of love,
He found himself encamped, and, 'midst its sweets,
Became bewildered by excess of joy.
To him it seemed an earthly paradise
Beyond the bounds of which he could not stray :
And that no noxious weed, or poison-flower,
Should ever blight, or taint, its purity
He most devoutly wished and ever prayed.

All-powerful love ! he owned thy sov'reign sway,
Thy welcome fetters bound him in delight ;
But to be near her, by her presence sunned,
He had endured the lowliest lot in life
And thought himself a Monarch crowned with bliss.
Absent from her, he nothing knew of joy :
The wheels of time were clogged, and only moved

With painful effort's dull and creaking sounds :
Then hours seemed days, and days as weeks appeared,
Then, though the skies were fair, he saw them foul—
The gloom within pervading all without—
Was ever heart so bound to heart as his ?
Did Love e'er venture on so deep a sea ?

O Love ! young Love ! how strong thou art when pure !
How beautiful when true—how angel-like !
Thine are the realms through which the Bird of Morn
Pursues its pleasures on a tireless wing ;
Thine are the splendours of their summer sun,
And thine the azure of their cloudless skies.
Thou wilt not leave thy cherisht home for earth
Save for the meaner wants of common life,
Then, on re-strengthen'd pinions bravely borne,
Away thou soarest to thy Heaven again !
Thou wouldést not the stern realities
That cling around this cold, material clime,
But the perennial sunshine, flowers, and song,
Of rapt Imagination's airy world !

NOBLE LOVE.

BOOK FOURTH.

TILL her he met, his barque unheeding flew
From shore to shore, yet never haven sought,
But once Love's anchor touched that golden strand
It never lost one sand-grain of its hold.
And were it well to garner all our hopes
In aught of Earth Evander's there had dwelt,
Nor feared that still resistless flood of Change
Which sweepeth o'er Affection's cherisht spots
And only leaves a ruined waste behind—
A lonely sepulchre of buried hopes.
"Take courage, heart," he said, "Sincerity
Can build a sea-wall strong as adamant,
Impregnable to every wave but death,
Which only enters that the soul, set free,

May blend its being, in a purer sphere,
With that affinity it found on Earth :
Death breaks no vows, exhibits no deceit,
And, whilst its shadows trace immortal joys,
For ever shapes its consolations thus—
' Our after-Life shall former bliss excel.' "

No gath'ring clouds presaged a coming storm,
No fitful gusts a hurricane foretold,
The social sun had never seemed more bright
Than when it smiled o'er Edith's natal day.
Alas ! alas ! that life and love should prove
So pregnant with disasters unforeseen !
The very words that Herbert thought must leap
Like welcome tidings into ev'ry heart
Around his table grouped in festive glee,
Smote Edith and Evander with dismay !
Yet, had they dared to breathe one little word
Against that marriage-bond, to him so dear,
The doting father, and the faithful friend,
Had spurned them both for ever from his heart.

Her tender nature swooned, though none wot why —
Save he, whose prudent grief no outlet found

But in the deep complainings of his soul—
" I never lov'd before !—I never knew
The burning anguish, and the madd'ning thrill,
Of blighted love's mysterious influence !
Its fitful fever never fired my blood,
Or scorcht my brain before—I never felt
This strange unrest that sways me to and fro,
Like an unrudder'd bark that dares to live
Upon a wild, tempestuous, landless sea !"

She never could be more to him than now,
The only idol of his earthly faith,
The planet of his life, go where he might—
Whose distant rays would glad another sphere,
Whose beauty would become another's joy.
The poet gives to fathers flinty hearts,
Yet Herbert thought himself a different man,
And would have proved a type of gentleness
Had not his priceless honour been at stake.
True, they could fly his sight, his home, his hearth,
And jointly dare whatever fate might yield—
Whilst their ingratitude, Man's blackest sin,
Drew down his curses, as it dug his grave.
Evander's heart was like the rock-built house—

That, when the tempest howled, and torrents foamed,
Defied the blast, and every surge withstood ;
And he elected now to test its strength
By Suff'ring's discipline—with his own hands
To bind the cords of his self-sacrifice.
Esteem not this the coinage of a brain
O'er-wrought, and steept in sentimental lore,
Or ravings of impetuous, ardent youth,
More fickle than the transient April sky—
Evander's mind had been matured by thought,
By self-reliance fully disciplined ;
In purpose clear, in resolution strong,
He counted up the cost, and was content
To peril all for his lost Edith's peace—
The goddess of his heart's idolatry !

Night after night he courted sleep in vain—
At length exhaustion pleaded with such power
That Nature's great Physician came at last
And bore him into Dreamland, far away :
A child again, upon his nurse's knee,
He gazed once more on those familiar walls
That shelter'd him throughout his tend'rest years:
This picture passed away, and, in its stead,

Appeared the dingy house in Crutchéd Friars,
Just as it seemed when first he Herbert met :
The quaint old Grange came next, and, by its porch,
Stood Edith, with an infant in her arms—
And, by her side, a man of comely mien
Who prattled fondly with his earliest born.
A snow-white Dove came flutt'ring through the trees
And percht on pensive Edith's trembling arm :
From 'neath its downy wing a letter peeped—
" For Edith "—and no superscription else—
They broke the seal in eager, anxious haste,
And but to make amazement more intense :
Within, upon a silken scroll, were traced
The outlines of a noble Doric pile,
Its front engraven thus, on ground of gold—
" Evander's Gift to Edith "—nothing more.

Evander never sought her home again,
But hailed the light of that eventful day
Which dawned upon his life of hopeless love—
Hopeless in consummation, yet, withal,
A pilgrimage not destitute of joy;
For well he knew that Edith's inmost soul
Enshrined his heart as her life's talisman :

Youth writes its vows of love upon the sand,
Maturer age engraves them on a rock.

Far o'er the sea, Evander took his way,
Self-exiled from the land he loved so well—
Far o'er the sea, with memories in his heart
That never on his manly face were writ—
Far o'er the sea, on one firm purpose bent,
Inspired by gratitude, and fanned by love.

Time, like the torrent of a mighty flood,
Impetuous ever, surgeth ever on,
And round about our globe, unheeded still.
The foam-bell hours maintain their ceaseless whirl—
To feed the mighty waters of the Past
And mingle with its sea of Memories :
O vast, O awful sea ! O dread abyss !
Whose ever-yawning depths have swallow'd up
The countless generations of our race,
With all their joys and sorrows, hopes and fears !

Mysterious Future ! the sustainer, Hope,
For ever points to thee with outstretcht arms,
And, with exulting voice, still " onward " cries :

Unfathomed Future! endless End!
What fate, when this world's time shall cease to be,
Hid in thy far recesses, still awaits
This human race—which for a something lives
That earth-life ne'er hath yielded, nor can yield,
For which the soul yearns even until death—?

Day after day, year after year, rolled on
And found Evander bound to Fortune's wheel,
Each revolution yielding rich reward.
Whence this prolonged and ever cheerful toil —
This strong endurance of a lonely man ?
Nor wife nor child nor kith nor kin hath he,
And yet he ever addeth field to field—
And ship to ship—a Crœsus of the East !

That dream had never left the Wand'rer's breast :
Far o'er the sea, safe cabined in his heart,
He bore it as a precious growth of Love
To plant, some coming day, on English soil :
That dream assumed a fixt reality
And fashioned forth the Mission of his life—
The dreamer was the faithful worker now,
And hence endurance, hence his fervent zeal.

Noble Love.

Far o'er the sea—he never sailed again !
He saw the shadows fall across his path—
He felt the touch of an arresting hand—
He knew his work was done, well done, at last—
So set his house in order, and lay down.

Far o'er the sea—Old England's heart was stirred
With an impulsive flow of gratitude—
They bore his body and his treasure home :
The first reposeth near that upland Heath
He loved so well—close to the kindly Grange—
The other, with his memory, is enshrined
Within a stately Doric Pile whose walls
Have sheltered thousands whom the waves of life
Threw back upon its strand—as helpless wrecks
Unfit to battle longer with the storm.
Such was the ending of Evander's dream,
And such the Noble Love to Edith given—
Such is the history of a Life well spent,
Emblazon'd in a deathless Heraldry !

THE LIGHT OF THE WORLD.

HE God-Man Christ who deified the Truth
And on the Cross enthroned His righteousness,
Hath dower'd this world of ours with Love Divine
And made accessible the Mercy Seat :
He drove the Priests of Vengeance from the fane
And scatter'd wide their instruments of doom —
He drew aside the veil with rev'rent hand,
And, in the Holiest of Holies, men
Beheld a Father in their dreaded God.

The Star that rested over Bethlehem
Yet sheds its rays of sacred glory there -
Outliving races, rules, and dynasties ;
And that wild rocky slope of Nazareth
Hath memories that through the Ages bloom
Defying every blast of unbelief.

A golden halo circleth gentle Olivet
Where fell the Manna of Immortal Love
Bedewed with Mercy and Goodwill to Man;
And round Jerusalem there floateth still
The odour of His wondrous sanctity!

His mission o'er, His Light, the Word, proclaimed,
Our great Exemplar passed away from Earth—
To wait and welcome such as overcame.
Thus, near His throne, great Victors in the strife,
Are ranged the moral Heroes of the Past—
A countless throng of earnest, Noble Lives,
Tow'ring, like Anaks, in the Courts of Heav'n,
With crownéd heads, enstarred and glorified,
That, God-like, flash, and burn, and shine—
God-like, as earth-bound souls of God conceive,
But, to the One in All, Omnipotent,
As motes that shimmer in the noonday sun.
The well-belovèd John is also there—
A glorified and chief beatitude—
He bears the emblem of the Christian faith,
And meekly eyes the Man who standeth near;
And Mary, once despised and rudely spurned,
Whose teardrops washed His travel-stainéd feet,

Is leaning safely on the Master's breast.
How fruitfully suggestive that array!
Beyond the reach of uninspired pen—
Beyond the pencil's almost living power—
Beyond Imagination's loftiest flight—
Out-distancing and far transcending all!

Year after year, Time's viewless flood rolls on,
And still the God-Man, Christ, is manifest—
A universal, boundless Influence
For ever striving in this motley world
To counteract the Evil life evolves—
A power, if not a spirit, hard to throw:
The Devil is a most convenient friend
When men are prone to follow wickedness,
And huge enough to carry tons of sin:
Poor Devil! what a tool we make of thee—
Thee and that ever ready Providence
Are very scape-goats to the sons of men:
Anointed Kaisers devastate and slay
Through confidential hints from Providence,
And give it all the glory—theirs, the gain;
While pulpit-seers discern its righteous hand
In ev'ry famine-field of blighted grain.

When will this worse than pagan darkness flee
Before the light of intellectual day ?—
Our Devils are but downward tendencies,
And our Good Angels, upward-guiding thoughts.

Light of the World ! Incarnate Love of God !
When first Thy dazzling glory men beheld,
A re-created Life from chaos sprung,
Clad in the beauty of Thy Holiness.
All old things yet shall find that newer Life—
The reign of terror prompted Sacrifice,
The law of " blood for blood," and " blow for blow."
Shall merge into and mingle with that Love
Whose first-fruits are Goodwill and Charity.
But, nathless, Evil still hath potent sway
And bars the upward progress of the Soul :
Evil will fall—the campaign but begins—
Our Christian World is yet in infancy—
Our Centuries are but as days to Him—
Our cycled Ages, swiftly passing years :
The Past, the Present, and the Future, sweep
Before His Mind as lightnings flash and die—
Time but existeth in the thoughts of Man.

The Darkness fiercely warreth with the Light—

A mighty conflict, raging evermore—
The trampling to and fro, the battle-clang,
The crashing thunder of gigantic strife,
Commingling with the deaf'ning roar of Time,
Whose every fleeting moment marks some stage
Of mighty warfare, host engaging host.

Brave warriors of the Cross, press nobly on!
Your love and truth at length shall overcome;
Your weapons are the Lessons that He taught,
And only strike to heal the wounds they make—
The vanquished smile, and kiss correction's rod.

O blameless Life! exemplified in Love—
Love glorified by Faith's simplicity,
There cannot fail a season when mankind
Shall comprehend Thy mission's glorious truth—
That Uprightness is parent of all Joy
And Fellow-Love the source from which it flows.

'Tis well to measure out and weigh the stars,
To flash mysterious voices round the globe,
To sound the ocean and to scan its depths,
To use the elements we may not curb:

To beautify a beauteous world with Art
And flood it with Imagination's streams,
To people it with Fancy's brightest forms
And charm it with the wand of Intellect :
But Science, Art, and Intellect decay
When merely creatures of the creature Man,
And but inherit lastingness when interwove
With aims that heav'nward yearn—and, yearning, soar.
The only Sunrise that shall flood the world
With all-enduring glory and delight
Must issue from the inner souls of men—
Still grov'lling in the darkness and the dust :
The fellest tyrants that embitter life
Exist in passions nourisht and caresst.

Let Dreamers dream their dreams Republican,
And build vain hopes on frail Equality,
Revealing visions, vague and purposeless,
In eloquent obscurity of words ;
The men of action must lay hands on Work,
Nor let it slip their hold, till, from the swamps
Of Ignorance and Selfishness shall spring
The golden fruitage of a true Elysium :
Then radiant glories, shed by truthful lives,

Shall glad the earth with mercy and goodwill—
Mingling their rays with those that downward stream
From Him whose smile is an Eternal Sun.

When Priests no more shall mystify the world
With puzzling dogmas from ambitious brains,
Each anxious for a founder's name and fame;
When all our Preachers Charity shall teach,
And, with Example, ev'ry Precept crown;
When Czars, and Emperors, and Peoples shall,
For its own sake, love righteous Uprightness;
When Kings and Governments shall serve, not rule,
And be exponents of a Nation's will;
When Nations shall be fitted to control
The servants they elect—by moral force
Of educated and ennobled mind;
When men shall only unto others do
What they desire may to themselves be done;
When all Christ's Golden Laws are Rules of Life
And universal as the blesséd air—
Then, only, shall the Cross have done its work,
And Love be manifest through God, the Light!

GLORY.

T HE love of Glory and the lust of Power
Have deluged Europe with a sea of blood—
The Orient also, and the mighty West—
And now, once more, our suff'ring sister-land
Is drencht with priceless floods of Life's red wine,
And strewn with ghastly heaps of mangled slain :
Poor, bleeding France ! we cannot choose but grieve
That ever thou didst wed the Corsican.

The Infant Century, with wond'ring eyes,
Beholds the Glory of a Consulate
Which crowns an Empire and an Emperor !
To greet the Conqueror's triumphal march
Illuminations flare from ev'ry house,
In strange devices wrought and many-hued,
Flashing their coruscations o'er the crowds

Assembling ev'rywhere along, or near,
The dazzling pageant's gaily-dizen'd route.
Far as the eye can reach, a myriad mass
Of life extends, dense as the grassy blades
Upon a dew-fed meadow, southern-sunn'd :
One moment, all is silence— but the next
Rolls out a mighty sea of surging sound
Whose crashing waves the throbbing city shake :
Again, and yet again, the deaf'ning roar,
Commingled ever with " Napoleon !"
" Gloire !" " Victoire !" " Marengo !" " Italie !"
The Consulate has Hohenlinden won,
Defied the Pope, re-strengthen'd Switzerland,
Proclaimed old " perfide Albion " for War,
Sent Beauharnois to Roma's classic soil,
Annexed Piedmont, and noble d'Enghien shot
Or murdered, let it be the honest truth—
And well deserves its Chief the Glory-g't
Whose regal lustre fired his daring soul :
Lieutenant—General—Consul—Emperor !

Defeat—Captivity—Heléna—Death !

Scene after scene is changed : now Louis reigns

Chicanery thrives well on money-bags,
And marriages are made in Spain, not Heaven !

.   .   .   .

Fear, Flight, Disgrace—pour Angleterre !

Vision of Visions ! Babe Republican !
Sweet toy of Soldiers, Poets. and Savants—
Dear idol of Montmartre and Batignolles—
The Power that France, through Paris, must obey—
The full-developed flower of Liberty—
Whose life is National for evermore !
Alas ! the day ! the beauteous, smiling Babe
With Death untimely meets, nay, has its throat
Cut i' the early morn before the drums
Are beat—because they will not, being slashed.

.   .   .   .

Cannon—Bloodshed—Prisoners—Curses—Quiet.

.   .   .   .

Imperial Glory, Plenty, smiling Peace—
Imperial Beauty, Wealth, and Piety !

Let us abjure the doctrine that success,
At any price, is Virtue—nor, henceforth,
With hopeful words like these, essay to quite
Efface the blood-stains of a Coup d'Etat :—

" Beautiful France ! romantic, smiling land !

" Each honest British heart now holds thee dear—

" O'erflows with purest love for thee and thine,

" And with fond rapture our alliance hails :

" Be this the dawn of lasting brotherhood—

" The re-risen Empire's best achievement,

" And the bright harbinger of Europe's peace !

" Foremost alike in Science and in Art,

" Valiant alike in arms by land or sea,

" Breathing, as 'twere, the very selfsame air,

" We surely brothers were by heaven ordained.

" Thy manhood on old England's breast was nurst,

" Napoleon ! and thy fair Eugenie's blood

" Flowed from our hardy Barons of the North,

" So 'tis most meet that in thy reign the bond

" Of union should be ratified in love.

" The strangest tale of history's romance

" Thou hast most gloriously realized,

" And given the lie to every hireling pen

" That dared with obloquy to link thy name.

" Press nobly onward in thy bright career,

" And thou shalt yet achieve for lovely France

" A greater Glory than thy Uncle could—

" Though his vast intellect still wrought and planned

" For her advancement on the rolls of Fame.

" Napoleon ! France ! be to your mission true,

" And cultivate with zeal the peaceful arts—

" Seize ye the golden hour that dawneth now

" And carve yourselves a name that shall endure

" When War's last trumpet shall have ceased to sound,

" And Earth is jubilant o'er lasting Peace !"

.   .   .   .

Vain dream ! the sword was only sheathed, not beat

Into the ploughshare of millennial peace—

The gold-bought Glory-cry has done its work,

And France is made to " slip " a yielding leash.

Both Crown and Crowd are drunken with a Past

Which it were well the world had never known :

The curse of Europe is again let loose—

Imperial Slaughter drives its car afield :

Envy and Lust postilion the steeds

Whose nostrils are dilate with scent of blood,

And Cæsar riots o'er the plains of death.

His mission now is to baptise with fire

The scion of a devastating race—

Whose name is writ in Glory and in Blood,
Whose monuments are bronz'd with human gore:
The evil brand is on another brow—
The damning seal that binds him hand and foot
To lustful conquest, fire, and sword, and death:
Will Heaven not rain its wrath on act so foul?
Is Earth not weary of the Slaughter-Fiend–
Of Human sacrifice at Glory's Shrine?
Must we look tamely on, with grieving hearts,
And see our fellows mowed like ripen'd grain
Before each God-anointed Man of Blood?

．　　　　　．　　　　　．

O fatal mission! worse than fatal end!
How thou hast dragged the Lilies through the mud
Of crushing failure and supreme defeat!
Better have left the Teuton in his lair–
To multiply his Cubs and thrive apace
On Federation and Philosophy.

Arise, Humanity! arise!—crush out
All " Right-Divine " that is in league with blood,
And re-create the nobler Right of Man
To cannonade with Moral Force alone:
Thus gentle Peace shall o'er the world preside
And Mercy be with Liberty enthroned!

THE SCOTTISH EMIGRANT.

AREWELL, dear Native Land, whose moun-
tains hoar

And storm-embracing hills, receding, fade :

Farewell, ye lakes and roaring cataracts—

Ye loupin' burns and silver-threaded rills—

Ye heath'ry knowes and gowan-studded leas—

Ye rocky glens and primrose-jewelled nooks—

Ye fertile straths and clover-scented fields—

To one, and all, a long and last farewell!

Dear Native Land—of Wallace, Bruce, and Burns—

Whose last dim outline slowly melts in space—

Should distance e'er erase thee from my heart,

Let me be branded as some son of Cain

Who fled a land he was unfit to grace—

Or one who for a promised pottage sold

The glorious heritage of memory !

There may be fairer lands, with brighter skies
That limn no clouds upon the lakes below -
And cast no giant-shadows on their hills—
But stouter arms and truer hearts are none.

Dear Native Land ! where'er my footsteps roam —
Whate'er the future of my life may be,
Thy every feature in my heart shall live
And prove a solace in the coming years.
Thy grand old memories shall visit me
Amid the mighty forests of the West,
Or on the distant praries' vast expanse ;
Thy sweet old songs shall gladden us at eve
When all our hearts, untravell'd, think of thee,
And to our children's children shall descend
The grandeur and the glory of thy name.

From rude beginnings thy career has ris'n
To be a theme among the nations round—
A constellation in the world of Fame—
A grand, enduring type of Liberty—
Of liberty obtained through fire and sword,
Of independence bought by blood and death !
As towers his shrine above old Snowdoun's plains,

A fitting monument for such as he,

So towered the noble Wallace in his life—

A power to lead, to conquer, and subdue—

A dread avenger of his country's wrongs,

An unrelenting scourge of tyranny :

Shock after shock his lion frame withstood,

Feud after feud his lion-heart defied,

Foe after foe he caused to bite the dust.

And hewed the way to crowning Bannockburn.

Came then the Bruce, fair Carrick's peerless peer.

To crush the proud invader and avenge

The foulest murder of a murderous reign —

The martyrdom of Scotia's darling son.

O chequered Past ! dread purgatorial years !

Your blood-drencht fields, your straths and fire-scathed
   pines,

May well grow green and bravely flourish now :

Such is the Christian's arduous fight of Faith,

That leads through fiery ordeals to the Cross—

But there he gains an everlasting crown !

Must I o'erleap the intervening years

Sore plagued with woes and internecine strife,

The crucial tests that order must forego,

Nor breathe the name that Scotland holds so dear—
Dear, though detraction level all its shafts,
Its venom-barbs, against a woman's breast ?
Ill-fated Queen ! the plaything of the hour—
The shuttlecock which rude conspirer's strove
To seize and bandy at their own behest.
He must be less than man who reads, unmoved.
The sadd'ning story of thy hapless life :
Poor, murdered Queen, thou'rt not the first, nor last.
Who sought for shelter and received a grave !
But while a halo gilds thy memory still,
Fit guerdon for the wrongs thou hadst to bear,
And fitting tribute to unrivall'd charms—
Thy august cousin's name is stained with blood.
And travels through a mire of certain shame.

Less wronged was he who bore the Stuart name
And found an easy way to Scottish hearts,
And lives, embalmed, in Scotland's sweetest songs—
The darling hero of the " Forty-five "—
Whose mild, chivalrous bearing, like a charm,
Lit up the maiden's eyes where'er he moved,
And lit the beacons on the watchful hills
To rally thousands round a hopeless cause
And one more bloody baptism give the soil.

Brave covenanting Fathers! noble Sires!
Your memories are engraven on the rocks
Where ye took refuge from the murd'rous bands
Let loose like bloodhounds on your hunted tracks ;
And on the moors, where ye defied their fangs,
There lingers still the solemn sound of praise
With which your souls were strengthen'd for the fight.
No alien church, no sporting priests, took root
In Caledonia's stern and rugged breast,
The heather was on fire, and, vermin-like,
They fled the North for more congenial skies :
Now, bless'd with peace, the frugal country thrives,
Though vested rights drive thousands far afield—
To plant the Thistle on earth's furthest shores.

And must I say farewell, dear Native Land,
To all thy lovely and romantic scenes ?
Shall I no more sweep down the noble Clyde
To greet the vast Benlomond's misty crown—
Or climb his rugged sides with panting breath ?
Or scale Dumbarton's rock-hewn steps to gain
A peep at far Benledi—and Venue ?
Is fair Loch Lomond lost to me for aye,
Sweet Inversnaid, and all its floating isles ?

The cave of bold Magregor, and the path
That leads to where Loch Katrine shining lies
Like a huge amethyst amidst the hills ?

Shall I no more the Cowal shores traverse—
Or skim along thy waters, dark Loch Fyne ?
Or see the phosphored herrings gleaming bright,
As the big night-haul lands them on the deck—
Gleaming, as if with glow-worms from the deep,
Or millioned diamonds from old Neptune's mines ?
Will beauteous Arran never lure me more——
To spots where I have spent my bridal days,
To lovely Rosa's Glen or Goatfell's feet ?
On Brodick Bay will I ne'er ply the oar—
Or tempt its timorous whitings with my bait
Or, landing, climb the Holy Island's brow
And hail grim Ailsa anchored out at sea ?

Shall Bonnie Doon no longer hear my voice
As o'er the Brig I chaunt the " Scots wha hae,"
And, with a reverential eye, behold
The temple consecrate to him who drove
His Plough of Song into the hearts of men,
And stirred the world to listen and obey

God's mandate of Equality in Man?

Brave-hearted Bard! not always like the lark

On verdant fields, or in the sunny sky,

Didst thou give utt'rance to the voice of Song—

But often 'midst the levin of the storm

That strung thy verse with words of living light

To brighten ever as the ages roll!

And shall I never more behold the sun

Rise in its splendour o'er the Braes of Mar,

Rolling his golden glory's lavish waves

Athwart their rugged sides and down the glens—

Till every bush of whin more golden grows,

And every stream like molten metal runs—?

And thou, Edina, dear to Scottish hearts,

Their chronicle and casket of the past—

The Queen of Scottish cities and the seat

Of all that intellect makes truly great—

Must I no more re-visit thy fair streets,

No more thy Calton hill or Castle see—

No more through Holyrood's deserted halls

Muse o'er the changing fortunes it hath known—?

To ancient Roslin shall I flit no more—

Where Genius gave all but life to stone—?

Or thence to famous Melrose, and the Tweed.
Where, 'midst the mould'ring pomp of priestly pride,
Old Dryburgh hath entombed the Wizard Bard?

Alas! no more!—around the bounding prow
I hear and see the separating waves
That cut me off for ever from thy shores,
My own, my much belovèd Mountain Land!

Once more, farewell!—the waters of my soul
Are swelling too, and like to drown my heart.
Dear Native Land! the ashes of my sires
Are mingled with thy soil, so dear to me;
And, more than all, beneath its turf are laid
Her dear remains who hath been more to me
Than mother to her bosom-tended babe—
More than the saintliest sister, or the kin
Who sweeten life with pure affection's flow:
My constant shadow and my substance she,
The life of all my living, and its joy—
The uncomplaining partner of its woe!

ROBERT BURNS.

I.

ILENT the harp of Scotia hung,
No one of joy or sorrow sung,
When from her peasant sons up-sprung
   The Minstrel Burns!

II.

He seized the harp with vigorous hand,
Each chord awoke at his command,
And song o'erflowed the slumbering land
   In "wood-notes wild."

III.

At home, afield, at night, or morn,
Behind the plough, or 'midst the corn,
His faithful Muse ne'er left forlorn.
   Her darling son.

IV.

She winged his thoughts with words of fire,
And breathed such music o'er his lyre
As made the listening world admire--
          In wonder lost !

V.

An inner harp, his noble heart—
Eolian-like—took many a part,
Yet ever from one note would start—
          That note was Love.

VI.

He had a tear for sorrow's tale—
Mirth that made mirth the more prevail—
A plaintive, dirge-like, deepening wail
          For mourning man.

VII.

By woman's smile supremely blest,
Love reign'd and revell'd in his breast—
A surging ocean of unrest—
          To calm unknown.

VIII.

If she, his -meanwhile— fairest fair,
But frowned, he sunk into despair,
And curs'd, as dire beyond compare,
    His adverse fate.

IX.

But when the coy or timorous maid
Once more her face in smiles arrayed,
Then, quick as thought, to deepest shade
    He banished care.

X.

Though ever, like th' unsated bee,
He, searching for fresh sweets, would flee.
One modest floweret most lov'd he—
    His " Mary dear."

XI.

At labour's close, where none might hear,
They strayed by some sweet streamlet near,
Each pouring in the other's ear
    A tale of love.

XII.

By day th' inspirer of his themes,
By night the angel of his dreams,
What wonder, Coila, though thy streams
            Of " Mary " sing?

XIII.

One holy morn, in hawthorn'd May,
They met, a fond adieu to say—
To meet upon their bridal day,
            Love jubilant !

XIV.

Between them flowed a limpid brook—
O'er which they held the HOLY BOOK—
And vowing Love till Death, they took
            A last farewell !

XV.

Ayr flowed serenely as before
Nor wist the tale its waters bore—
Yet to be read, as classic lore,
            In days to come.

XVI.

Alas! that bridal bell ne'er rung,
No bridal ode for her he sung,
Nor ever, with his manly tongue,
   Did call her " wife."

XVII.

O faithful Love!--O cruel Fate!
Why from our song-bird tear his mate?
Why scatter bliss so truly great,
   And yet so brief?

XVIII.

Relentless Death! why to the gloom
And cold caresses of the tomb
Consign her youth's unfaded bloom—
   And pierce his heart?

XIX.

Familiar strains on every tongue,
The sweetest ever mortal sung,
Like pearls upon her love he strung—
   Song's brightest gems!

XX.

That " ling'ring star with less'ning ray,"
O how it steals the heart away—
As if it would the soul convey
   To brighter skies !

XXI.

Strange ! how a lowly highland Maid
Could so his inmost heart invade—
That till he low in death was laid,
   She linger'd there !

XXII.

And still increasing with his fame
Shall be the halo round her name
Who, even lost, was still the same—
   His morning star.

XXIII.

O chequered life ! Edina now
With holly wreath adorns his brow,
Wit, Beauty, Rank, and Fashion bow
   Before the Bard :

XXIV.

Now -armed with rod, book, pen, and ink–
He's taking notes of strong " Scotch Drink,"
And told " to act. but not to think,"—
                    Poor Poet BURNS!

XXV.

Thus he. like great Apollo, made
His way through mingled sun and shade,
And many Cyclops low he laid—
                    With satire keen.

XXVI.

O for the magic of his pen—
That so enthralled the hearts of men—
Then might we tell how deep his ken
                    Of human life !

XXVII.

Heroes have been who never drew
The sword of death, or foemen slew—
Of such was BURNS, hence tyrants knew,
                    And felt, his power.

XXVIII.

He wielded but a truthful pen—
So truthful, that the hearts of men
Were willing captives of each strain
    That from it flowed.

XXIX.

Of " honest poverty " he sung
In words that made the old feel young—
And with new life the heart re-strung
    Of pining youth.

XXX.

He made them feel that sense and worth
Might cope with titles or with birth,
And how, ere long, o'er all the Earth,
    Love should preside !

XXXI.

The meanest things to him were dear—
The " daisy " of the opening year—
The "timorous beastie " in its fear—
    And " Mailie, dead."

XXXII.

Keen as the hawk, mild as the dove,
His heart o'erflowed with human love,
And Truth—bright effluence from above—
        Imbued each word.

XXXIII.

Far out upon the trackless sea,
The sailor's heart is filled with glee
While singing some sweet melody
        Of Scotland's Bard.

XXXIV.

And, sailing from their mountain land,
While fades her fast receding strand,
Sad exiles chaunt—a plaintive band—
        '' Ye Banks and Braes.''

XXXV.

The soldier on the battle field
Oft nerves his arm the sword to wield,
And makes his breast his country's shield,
        Through '' Scots wha hae.''

F

XXXVI.

On prairies vast, in forests deep,
Where Scotia's sons home-vigils keep,
Wi' ROBIE BURNS they laugh and weep
                    To suit the hour.

XXXVII.

At home, abroad, in house, or mart,
Within the People's mighty heart—
That ne'er can with its minstrel part—
                    Is BURNS enshrined!

XXXVIII.

O'er every sea his fame hath flown,
From pole to pole—from zone to zone –
His ev'ry word and act made known—
                    Familiar things.

XXXIX.

A fruitful theme for countless lays,
Earth still is vocal with his praise
Whose genius sheds its dazzling rays
                    O'er every land.

Robert Burns.

O could his spurners meet him now
From whom they turned with haughty brow-
Who bore the Harp behind the Plough—
                    The Prince of Song !

A censured life—a ceaseless moil—
Sore dashed with care and slavish toil :
A sun flower on a rocky soil
                    He lived—and died :

No ! still he lives ! BURNS cannot die !
Although inurned his ashes lie,
That truth-lit fame still mounts on high—
                    Bright'ning for aye !

FALLEN.

MOTHER, lay me on my bed.
　　There to rest my weary head,
Nor take me thence till I am dead—
　　My spirit far away, mother.

There is a weight upon my brain,
And in my head a ceaseless pain—
I'll never know sweet peace again
　　Till life hath closed on me, mother.

" What, O what doth ail thee, child?
And why those words and looks so wild?
Hath sin my long lost daughter soiled?
　　" Tell me, dearest do, Mary!"

O mother! had you heard him cry,
Or seen upturned to me his eye—
As heaven received his parting sigh,
　　You then could read my grief, mother.

O God ! it was a fearful thing !
So young, so fair, so flourishing—
Death now no woe to me can bring,
 No deeper woe than that, mother !

" Rest thee, rest thee, sleep awhile—
Foot sore, and heated with thy toil,
A fevered brain doth sense beguile,
 And fancies fill thy brain, Mary."

O mother ! would that it were so !
I'd rather ever raving go
Than feel the truth of what I know—
 As now I feel it, here, mother !

'Twas not the long and weary miles—
'Tis not that fever sense beguiles—
But deep and damning sin that piles
 Its crushing weight on me, mother !

" Almighty God ! O grant me grace !
And, if Thou canst, her sin efface—
O Father ! do not hide thy face !—
 I'll listen to thee now, Mary."

Fallen.

For many a month, my mother dear,
When he had borne me far from here,
I headlong ran guilt's wild career—
    Forgot my God, and thee mother:

Then God forgot—then came the blow,
The curse, the spurn, and laid me low,
And then that hapless child of woe—
    The sinless fruit of sin, mother.

" I tremble, dearest, for the rest,
Say he was cherisht, lov'd, caresst—
Say that he died upon thy breast—
    A drooping flower from birth, Mary ! "

O mother ! mother ! would he had !
Such blest release had made me glad,
But when I did it, I was mad,—
    O mother ! pray for me—mother !

Mother ! mother ! pray for me !—
His voice I hear—his face I see—
O God ! but this is agony—
    Kiss ! kiss me !—ere I die – mother

WON AND LOST.

S OME one and twenty years ago the warmth
    Of Love's delightful fever thrilled my veins :
Then ev'rything seemed bathed in magic light
If one sweet presence only lent its smile,
Then darkness, pall-like, overhung the world—
That was, in truth, no world—without that sun :
How far Love's glorious landscape stretcht its lines,
Beneath an azure cloudless and serene,
Into that radiant future hope foretold !

Nor did I sing in vain—to listless ears—
My simple lays a genial welcome met,
And ere another Autumn gathered in
Its laden sheaves, I wedded with my love :
Through one score years of Life's contingencies
We joyed and sorrowed on, and then—she died.
With busy hands and still more busy brains

We toil incessantly throughout the years,
Yet gather nothing up that can prolong
Existence, or outbid the Lord of Life.

To that most ancient of heart histories,
Love's consummation and Love's empty shrine,
How much have I to add of light and shade?
Perhaps not more, or less, than most of men,
If, business-like, the average were struck—
But I know that I know, and what I feel:
I know that evermore there is a void
Within my heart that never can be filled,
And feel there is a presence ever near,
Impalpable to touch, to vision void,
Encircling this my soul and all its thoughts
As doth the atmosphere mine outer man:
Its spirit-motion seems to move the air
Like Zephyr's faintest sigh at summer-eve
Or infant breathings in a stilly room—
Nor may I stir beyond it if I would.

That change of living form which we call Death
Which leadeth all that's lovely to decay—
Hath not the power to break the chains of Love

Or shake the hope of truer Life to come :
Yet earth's duality of day and night,
Its ever fluctuating calms and storms,
Its strange unrest and unprogressive whirl,
But typify the life of creature-man :
The something hoped for never satisfies,
There ever is a vacuum to be filled.

Fame is a mirage that enchants a while,
Yet faileth to refresh the thirsty soul
When it hath reached the desert sands of age ;
And Wealth, the glist'ning pebbles of the beach
Which eager children gather all the day—
Yet leave behind when homeward they return :
God and the Spirits only can us bring,
Through Death, to their enduring oases
Of heavenly rest and satisfying joy.

ALBERT THE GOOD.

OBIT. DECEMBER, MDCCCLXI.

———

BENEATH an avalanche of sudden woe,
    A crushing weight of sorrow unforseen,
The mighty heart of England bleeding lies:
A glory hath departed from her midst,
The pillar of her Throne is rent in twain,
And Death holds sov'reign sway o'er all the land.

There is no fitting tongue for grief so great,
No words wherewith to clothe so dire a blow
As that which now hath smote the country's breast:
The Kingliest Man she ever saw is dead—
The kindliest heart she ever knew is still!

A surging sea of sorrow Europe fills,
And o'er the world shall far extending flow

Albert the Good.

In countless streams of undisguised regret :
No splendour borrowing from rank or power,
He added lustre to the British Crown,
And dignified its greatness by his worth.
His brief, yet bright career, for ever closed,
Shall henceforth be a model for such men
As would be truly great like him we mourn :
A fulness of urbanity and grace,
A blandly courteous, gentle, winning mien,
A cultivated mind with riches stored,
A princely patronage of peaceful arts,
A deep devotion to our native land,
Crowned his domestic virtues—shrined in Love!

Weep world, weep audibly, when good men die,
And give thy sorrow unrestrainéd voice :
'Tis fit that lamentations should be heard
When from Worth's firmament a guiding star
Of gen'rous influence fades and disappears :
Void darkness marks the orbit where it moved,
And, evermore, there is a solemn sense
Of hopeless desolation in the soul—
Which but corrodes itself with vain regrets :
We almost question Heav'ns sagacity

To thus permit the world's impov'rishment,
And dare to think ourselves the things of Chance.

The social life of England's millions wore
No aspect of ennobling life till he,
With thoughtful foresight and refinement rare,
Saw Britain's greatness in developed Mind,
And, straightway, bent him to the welcome toil
Which gave our age quaint Chaucer's House of Glass—
More wondrous strange than even he conceived.
Its influence flashed beyond our sea-girt Isle,
And, near and far, Earth's slumb'ring sons awoke
To Art-Religion, with unmaiméd rites,
And aspirations which exalt the Mind
Beyond the crave of sensual appetite—
To throne it in the inner souls of men.

For many a joy-reft one she oft hath grieved
Whose royalty is now the seat of woe,
And many a tear she striven hath to dry
Who now herself must weep heart welling tears:
If mortal consolation aught avail
In such an hour of deep, unfathomed grief,
A Nation's sympathy is wholly thine—
Our dearly lov'd, bereaved, and widow'd Queen.

ON THE CLYDE

I CANNOT well but love thee, noble Firth !
Near whose familiar strand my place of birth——
A sweetly nestled cottage, fair to see—
Smiled forth, half hid amongst rich greenery
Of graceful birch, gnarl'd oak, and palm-like pine,
With hedge of thorn, sweet briar, and eglantine.
Huge masses of grey rock lay on the shore,
And granite boulders which the icebergs bore
From Northern coasts—how many years ago ?
On these—o'er these—I have leapt to and fro,
And in and out the pools that 'midst them lay,
From dawn till dusk, how many-a, many-a day ?

These hills are just the well-known hills of yore,
That spacious river shineth as before—
There are the rugged cliffs on which I played——
Here the bright pebbly beach on which I strayed :

I see the lowly cottage by the wood
Still nestling in its leafy solitude:
The blue smoke still in filmy wreaths ascends,
And still around the hearth may mingle friends·
But not the early loved, the lost, the true,
The dearest joys my childhood ever knew !

Beauty's blithe spirit breathes divinely here,
Clothing in smiles the landscape far and near :
Dumbarton's ancient twain-cleft rock I see—
A noble monument of ancient chivalry—
Below, the shores of Cardross and Ardmore
Bask in the sunbeams as in days of yore:
The smiling village next, with life a-throng,
Enlivens the fair scene—just as the song
That follows a rich, eloquent display
Yields a fresh charm, nor drives the old away.
Embosomed in a forestry of green,
The Ardincaple turrets here are seen—
Confronting modestly the bolder towers
Argyll hath reared above the lovely bowers
Of fair Roseneath—that simply sweet retreat
Where Nature's richest charms, commingling, meet.

Inlets and bays indent Kilcreggan shore,

Where smugglers oft their hard-earned booty bore:

Lochlong is opening up—as round I gaze—

Its rugged peaks, hid by the morning haze,

Sublimely tower above the point of Strone—

O'er shores, once bare, now fully flanked with stone

Close packed, in one long range, the villas stand,

Some rattled up at random—others, planned:

Kilmun, I know, lies snugly round the way,

Frequented still, though rather in decay:

Sandbank, on Hafton shore, the eye can reach

Its mimic mansions and its long flat beach:

Below, the Lazaretto house still stands,

Though some rude knaves, with sacrilegous hands,

Have pulled the quaint old Lazaretto down

To form upon its site a villa-town—

But no " old Gordon " now doth ply the oar

To row as in a trice from shore to shore:

O matchless panorama! rich in charms!

Gazing on thee the Wand'rer's bosom warms—

While thoughts of the old time steal o'er his heart

And whisper, " Childhood is life's better part."

MOMENTOUS QUESTIONS.

WHY art thou happy ? why content,
    When there are sown for thee in ripening fields
    The Tares of separation in their yields?
    Thy happiness is only lent
To render its withdrawal worse to bear,
And make thee feel a more intense despair.

    One common lot—one common road,
Though numberless its lanes and byepaths be,
Is trodden by foredoomed Humanity :
    Rush wildly on, or slowly plod,
Before thee there is but that Death-crowned goal
Which bounds the last earth-effort of the soul.

    Hence, all that vain and foolish pride
Which joyeth only in the World's caress,
And empty blandishment, is foolishness :
    Let true Philosophy with man abide.

And teach him what a helpless worm found Earth
In that frail thing he is, death-sown at birth.

　　Our Love is Passion's Selfishness,
Which simply seeketh what it likes or needs
To satisfy its longings and its greeds,
　　So clingeth fast to Earthliness :
Than which no more delusive food doth grow
To cheat the appetite with empty show

　　Of seeming nourishment—
Yet satisfieth not, nor ever can,
The daily wants of the immortal man.
　　What reck we Punishment
From age to age, from sire to son,
Since motley Time its race began to run ?

　　Man still is happy, still content,
Ev'n sitting in that cell of the condemned,
His inward heart, whose walls are girt and hemmed
　　By Death's dark armament
Of bristling evils and close-ambushed woes—
Which, day by day, around him nearer close.

But are men happy in that mood
Which chaseth leav'ning sorrow from the sight,
And out of ruin buildeth fresh delight
　　　To cheat Joy's early widowhood ?—
Masking the spreading leprosy of care
With garments fitted for the leper's wear.

　　　Some live on Hope, esteeming life
A wondrous web as yet to be unrolled—
That may be richly wrought with pleasure's gold—
　　　And wherefore on tempestuous strife
Of sorrow uncontrolled should such embark ?
Or leave Hope's dazzling sunshine for the dark ?

　　　.　　　　.　　　　.　　　　.

　　　Why happy, Christian, if set free
From actual agony of flesh and bone ?
Or such soul sickness as doth wring the moan
　　　From frail humanity ?
" 'Tis not because I more than others know,
But that, when thirsting, to the Fount I go : "

"I nothing know but that I am,
And feel that prescience is no gift of man ;
Nor can content me with that seer-like plan
  Which some audacious giant-sham
Hath in a fit of pious fraud unfurled—
Fixing a time to blast the used-up world.

"Christ is that Fountain of the Soul
Whose satisfying waters can assuage
Its hottest thirst—or quell the fever's rage
  That brooks no touch of earth-control :
Their healing virtues, fraught with heavenly balm.
Inspiring hope and shedding holy calm.

"The only refuge of the heart
When Time's vicissitudes their shadows cast
O'er transient joys, too rapturous to last,
  Existeth in life's better part—
Where active virtues with meek Faith combine,
And in the Light of His example shine."

LIFE IN EARNEST.

Inscribed to the Memory of the Rev. James Hamilton, D.D.

———

INGER not in lanes of sorrow,
    Sigh not midst their leafless trees,
Man must live for a to-morrow
Till the Master-mind decrees
Higher life than is the human—
Higher love than that of woman.

Misanthropic doubtings never
Guide to Wisdom's high estate,
But experience showeth ever
That they but embitter Fate—
Till aside from Virtue's gateway
The poor doubter turneth straightway.

Once within Sin's gloomy portals,
All the light of life is gone,

All the love that blesseth mortals,
And he feeds on Vice alone—
Burning food that breedeth fever
In each tortured unbeliever.

Leave the haunts of senseless folly !
Where no summer of the soul,
With its aspirations holy,
Cometh from their wretched dole—
And in path's of honest duty
Life will gain undying beauty.

Tarry not till it is later,
Downward steps await the feet
Of the doubting Virtue-hater—
While congenial vices meet
In the soul-o'erwhelming ocean
Of a wasted life-devotion.

O believe that Life is earnest !
Be not to Inaction given—
Yet, in working, see thou learnest
How to mount the stairs of Heaven :
For the soul that truly winneth
On the Earth its Heav'n beginneth.

MEN OR MONKEYS?

—

SO men are merely monkeys after all—
    The fat and dumpy, and the lean and tall—
The young, the old, the rich, and eke the poor,
The king, the lordling, and the muddled boor—
At least we come from monkeys Darwin says,
And I confess to many monkey-ways
In men and women too—both old and young—
The monkey-antics and the monkey-tongue.
The tails continued, as continuations,
Might have been useful in some occupations;
For monkey-folly largely we inherit,
With all too little of his Tail-ship's merit;
And monkey-foolery we ape right well—
Although we have no tails whereof to tell.

Success to Monkey-dom! it gains prestige—

Some day 'twill crown a monkey as lord-liege,

One who will hold his court, and his levee,

Where tailor's tails may float in fancy free.

I never more will visit our grand *Zoo*

Without that deference to monkeys due—

Lamenting o'er the curse of disen-tail

Which hath made poor humanity so frail,

For—pray let us be serious for a minute—

I do believe there was a something in it ;

In what ?—the tail ?—yes, frankly, I believe

That mankind o'er the loss of tail should grieve :

Adam was but an ape who, when he fell,

Lost ev'ry " Vestige " of his guiding tail ;

And man no longer is a thoroughbred—

He has no tail to guide his erring head.

Eve saw, no doubt, that it might prove a flail,

And so agreed that Man should lose his tail ;

And Satan also had some end in view

When he made up that cunning apple stew :

If that confounded apple caused th' uproar

Why were not apples rottened evermore ?

Yet miserable man will apples eat

Though 'twas their beauty strengthen'd Eve's deceit :

Henceforth, let apples be eschewed and shunned,

And he who grows them mercilessly dunned—
No wonder that the Monkeys love them so
When they exalted Apes to sink Men low—
Throw apples to the monkeys, or the dogs,
Who still have tails to wag—or to the hogs !

What's in a tail ? some ask—a something, surely,
Else Adam had not felt so shocking poorly :
He cut his stick, but had no tail to turn,
'Twas wholly gone, and " Man was made to mourn."
The tail was gone—and I, its tale who tell,
Can but conceive that it from Adam fell—
While Satan planned the whole affair that he
Earth's Chief Gorilla should in future be :
He, since the hour when 'twas by Adam lost,
Has been possessor of the monkey-boast—
And this is all that I have learnt from thee,
No tittle more, O Darwin the-orie !

But worse exists than semi-monkey fun
In those by loss of tail unmanned, undone—
Such madly riot through guilt's wild career,
And neither God, nor man, nor devil fear.
Do monkeys ever play the pranks of men

Who lie and swindle for the love of gain—
Who, one day with their feet beneath his table,
The next, will cheat a friend—if they are able—?
All's fair in business, as in love or war,
In coal or cotton, tallow, hemp, or tar ;
In all commodities—in scrip or shares—
In barren mines, or other nests of mares :
Freight the prospectus, like a clipper trim it,
And clench the money by a prudent " Limit."
Or teach a Sunday-school, and preach goodwill,
The while you rob a blinded master's till ;
Or, higher game, build to your name a church—
Which means, " my creditors are in the lurch."
Do monkeys ever soak their brains with gin,
The curse of England and the nurse of sin ?
Or add fresh fuel to the per'lous stuff
Which never burns inebriate-throats enough ?
Or weight the scales that holds the poor man's bread—
Cheating the mouths so eager to be fed ?
Or, with adult'rous compounds, sow the seed
Of fell disease—for very devil's greed ?
Or, for a contract of good honest cloth,
Plant shoddy-waddy, ready for the moth ?
Such men are princes in the course of time,

And die embalmed in eulogies sublime--
Their names are handed *down*—I won't say *where*—
While titled beggars woo each wealthy heir.
Do monkeys pulpits mount, with saintly grace,
When fresh from orgies that would apes disgrace?
Or boast a lineage, measured by the mile,
While tempting woman with a Judas-smile?
Or ply seduction without let or fear?
Or murder babes by thousands ev'ry year?
Or stake and lose a fortune in a day—
On gambling race-course, or in hidden play?
Or patronise the hells we won't put down?
Or make " Anomyma " the thing " in Town ? "

Could monkeys, rudder'd monkeys, e'er do so?
No, monkeys have not fallen quite so low—
'Tis with the semi-monkey, shorn of tail,
That common sense and higher reason fail—
Place Man and Monkey, Man is sure to win
The race of Folly for the goal of Sin!

LET THERE BE LIGHT.

(JANUARY, 1869.)

———

ET us not pursue the Shadow
  While we let the substance pass,
And, with all our love of profit,
  Be eschewing gold—for brass.

Still the counterfeit is current,
  And things are not what they seem :
We are fed. but are not nourisht—
  Finding much of life a dream.

Acting takes the place of action—
  Resolutions melt like snow—
And the evils we complain of
  Do but more unwieldy grow.

While we tend the brute creation
  With a still increasing care,
The poor Arabs of the nation
  Worse than kennell'd spaniels fare.

Heedless of their souls—immortal,
  Of their bodies— like to ours,
We deny them food or culture,
  Growing weeds in place of flowers.

Let us aid existing action,
  But let our demand be plain—
That, throughout this British nation
  NONE IN IGNORANCE REMAIN.

Yet when tongues have learned the lesson—
  Over words to nimbly run,
And the hands to write and cipher—
  There will still be much undone.

Routine learning is but framework
  For the clothing of the mind—
By the sterner work of training
  We must elevate our kind :

Man must know himself completely,
  By the light of moral laws—
By the truths that dwell in Nature—
  And discern effect from cause.

He must feel a self-reliant
  And a self-protecting man :
Safely armour'd o'er with knowledge—
  Pressing forward to the van.

Man's self-help is an innateness—
  An impulse by nature given—
And if guided through the darkness,
  It will find the light from heaven.

What a glorious achievement—
  What a victory to secure—
If this constant gravitation
  To the WORKHOUSE we could cure !

Why should pauperism flourish
  In this highly-favoured land ?
Yet till Ignorance be routed
  They will still go hand in hand :

Mark the drunkenness and outrage
  That from want ot culture spring—
See the filth, disease, and misery,
  That like serpents round us cling ;

While by thousands babes are slaughter'd—
    Through neglect, or want, or crime—
Stamping out the tender mercies
    Of this much-enlighten'd time.

Save, O save the young and helpless!
    Do not lose both hands and hearts—
Do not squander skill and labour
    That might swell our mighty marts.

Effort, now, is but a conflict
    With the adverse forces round—
For some oracles of progress
    Give a most uncertain sound:

And with sophistry prevailing,
    In great " leaders " of the day,
We must mould our own opinions
    Or, perchance, be led astray.

There are many platform Christians
    Who pass want and squalor by—
Or, with scant commiseration,
    See our prostrate thousands die:

Yet we are not seared or heartless,
But to habit very slaves—
Whose supineness grows to action
Digging many pauper graves.

We must grapple with such evils—
Springing from neglected roots—
Very upas-plants of Ignorance,
Bearing only deadly fruits.

Let the cry be " Education,"
Urged by patriotic tongues—
Giving voice to exhortation
With the power of British lungs !—

Give it freely and unfetter'd,
Free and open as the day,
And let no Denomination
Place obstructions in the way.

Close the pit-fall of Permission,
Level up the " ifs " and " buts,"
Else the Chariot of Progression
Will be landed in the ruts.

Cease to war about Religion,
 Which belongs to other spheres,
Where example hallows precept
 And to Home or Church endears :

Thus the Light will dawn triumphant—
 Thus the scales fall from the blind—
And the Future be ennobled
 By the onward march of Mind !

FADING.

ADING away,
　　Fading away,
Slowly but surely
　　Worketh decay.

　　A rose in June
　　Blossomed too soon—
Drooping and dying—
　　Death were a boon.

　　Friends !　O how few
　　Prove to her true !—
Death do not tarry,
　　She sighs for you.

H

Weary, weary,
Dreary, dreary,
The hours pass away—
Still He's near thee.

Poor—fatherless—
Weak—motherless—
Joy in believing,
Lord, give her this !

Ever, ever,
Comfort-giver,
Till her earth-eye close
Be thou with her.

Beyond the sky,
The keener eye
Of the soul escaped
Will then descry

A path of light
To glory—bright
Spirits in waiting,
Robed in pure white :

Praising the Lord—
With one accord—
Who the trembling soul
Will help afford.

Fear not, maiden,
He hath said in
His Holy Word, " Come
Heavy laden,

" Come unto me—
My grace is free—
I will give thee rest—
O come and see !"

Yes, that frail bloom
Speaks of the tomb,
But thou shalt never
Know of its gloom.

Dust unto dust,
Dust unto dust,
The purest's impure—
Life-pride—eye-lust.

But thou art free !
He died for thee,
And heaven shall be thine-
Eternally !

Farewell ! to meet
In converse sweet—
Near the great white throne—
At Jesus' feet :

Fading away,
Fading away—-
Like a morning star
Into bright day !

FIVE HUNDRED.

HE spirit-winds are bringing
    Sad music from the sea,
As if the waves were singing
    Some good ship's elegy—
How plaintive is the melody
    Those viewless couriers bear !
Floating through the mist and gloom—
O'er the hapless sailors' tomb—
    Listen, let us hear :

" At the break of day, there lay
    On the blue water's breast—
Like a sea-bird on its way
    Taking momentary rest—
A ship, whose ample, snowy sails

All idly flapping hung,
Waiting for the lagging breeze
That on shore among the trees
Playful roved and sung :

" When Old Neptune, shouting loud,
Piped it away to sea—
' That ship ! go, whistle in every shroud –
Obey ! thou knowest me !'
Sullenly growling, it blew—
Drew down a thunder-cloud—
And out to the ship both flew
With a hoarse and wild halloo !
As the sea they ploughed.

" Five hundred noble-hearted
On that ship's deck did stand—
Brave hearts who would have parted
With life for Native Land :
Proud was each hardy sailor,
And high each stout heart beat,
For their ship was no trailer
In the track—none might rail her,
Still the first of the fleet !

" But they did not like the land
　　Still looming o'er the sea—
That the breeze would bear a hand,
　　Each praying fervently.
They were out to fight the French,
　　And they wished to be the first
Who should meet the hated foe—
Still the sails swung to and fro,
　　And the calm they curst !

" Oh ! that men will thus forget
　　That they may not command,
But submissively await
　　The workings of His hand :
Scarce had murmuring begun,
　　When dark the heavens grew,
And a gloom like midnight's spread
For miles round the vessel's bed,
　　And o'er her bold crew.

" The breeze, still gath'ring strength,
　　Reached the ship—a wild gale—
And its fury poured, at length,
　　On each mast, in each sail :

It lashed me until I foamed—
   Mad-like it made me bound
With the good ship on my breast
Which but lately there did rest,
   Till they cried, ' One drowned !'

" Then, a moment slept its wrath,
   It let forth not a breath,
But I knew that in its path—
   Just behind—there lurked death.
With a blast that shook the heav'ns
   It burst o'er me again—
The vivid lightning flying !
The thunder quick replying !—
   Hail fell thick as rain !

" Over the side went each mast,
   Rigging, and sails, and spars—
Away they went, while, aghast !
   Looked on the stricken tars.
From the steersmen life had fled,
   None went to fill their place—
Though conscious of rocks a-head,
Powerless stood those living dead—
   Horror in each face !

" She struck !—bounded off again !—
     That cry which clove the air !—
Five hundred death-doomed men
     Breathing their soul's despair !
Again ! and again she struck !
     The keel snapped like a reed :
And down through the rent ship then—
Down—down came those living men
     The blue shark to feed !

" This was the work of an hour—
     Such hours are dreadful to me—
When the storm-wind comes in power
     I heave with agony !
I toss ships up and around,
     Like playthings on my breast,
And seldom repose have found
Till many, or all, were drowned—
     I rest, with their rest !"

FORSAKEN.

WELL, wed thee with another love,
    And let her bear thy name—
Say marriages were made in heaven—
    Say thou art not to blame.

Say thou didst never give me cause
    To think thy heart was mine :
That as a brother thou didst love—
    No other feeling thine.

Breathe honied whispers in her ear,
    The while her head doth rest—
Confidingly and lovingly—
    As mine hath—on thy breast.

And with thine arms around her thrown,
Thine eyes fixed on her face—
The mirror of the soul within—
Seek there her thoughts to trace:

To thy bosom press her—closer—
And while beneath thy glance
Her eyelids droop, kiss her warm lips
Till she, in love's sweet trance

All fearless sinks, revealing thus
Her wish to rest—sweet rest!—
For ever there, for ever so
To be by thee caresst!

Forget me, then—forget how oft
My head, like hers, hath lain
Upon thy breast, while thou didst vow
We'd never part again!

Forget me then, and—if thou canst
Be happy—happy be;
But deal more faithfully by her
Than thou hast dealt by me.

If ever—in some thoughtful hour
　Of searching solitude—
When o'er th' events of former days
　Repenting thou dost brood—

My memory with a frown should rise,
　Fear not! my lips are sealed :
From henceforth to my dying day
　Nothing shall be revealed!

And I forgive thee—all forgive !—
　Can I forget? O! never!
I, willow-like, o'er blasted hopes,
　Must droop, and sigh, for ever!

THE MARINERS.

LOVE the gallant mariners that travel o'er the
deep,

'Mid storm, in breeze, or hurricane, through ocean's
waves they sweep.

Though lightnings glare around him, and heaven's wild
thunders roll,

Unshrinking stands the mariner—undaunted is his soul!

No dangers pale his manly cheek, or dim his watchful
eye,

No tremblings seize upon his heart while wars the angry
sky :

But 'midst the jarring elements sails fearlessly and
brave—

The boast of proud Britannia—the warrior of the wave !

No calm, unbroken slumberings — no undisturbed repose—
Await the gale-tossed traveller at day's returning close :
Though darkness veils the silent earth, and shrouds the vasty deep,
Ev'n then the hardy mariner his careful watch must keep :

But, even then, his buoyant heart is full of mirth and glee
As, pacing round the dusky deck, he whistles to the sea;
Or tells of battles lost or won to cheer his listening mates—
Their bright eyes glowing brilliantly as o'er them he dilates.

And though no flowers of language deck, true eloquence adorns
Those tales of strife on ocean's fields—where sound no trumpet-horns—
Where no strains of martial music stir on the gallant band :
Nought fires them but their battle-flag and thoughts of native land !

Anon relieved, the hammock-bed receives his brawny
 form,
Then dreams he oft of foreign lands, of danger and of
 storm ;
Of childhood's home, youth's happy days, and scenes of
 early joy,
When first embarked he roved the seas a merry sailor
 boy !

  .   .   .   .

Bound homeward by the favouring gale, his heart beats
 wild and free
As perched upon the towering mast, and gazing o'er
 the sea,
He marks the cliffs of Albion rise proudly to his view—
A scene that oft in distant climes unfading memory
 drew.

Elate with joy he gains the deck, while swift the ship
 glides o'er
The fast receding, crested waves, and nears his native
 shore ;

Love-beaming eyes and rosy lips already meet his
    sight—
The ardent kiss, affection's boon, in fancy breathes
    delight—

Home! happy home! with all its joys, at last the wan-
    d'rer gains—
Imagination's dreams are fled—reality now reigns:
The welcome smile—the glowing kiss—reward the gal-
    lant tar—
From perils free, no adverse gales his Pleasure-voyage
    mar.

STARVED TO DEATH.

WEARILY, drearily, comfortless,
A girl sank down on a hard mattress,
While the golden light of a summer morn
Mockingly smiled on the poor forlorn.

Mockingly! said I ? yes, it was so,
A hollow smile o'er a scene of woe :
A garret, all furnitureless and bare—
Save some prized relics of earthenware,
An ancient stool, and the old arm-chair

Where the lone one's father had breathed his last,
Batter'd and worn by many a blast :
Fighting for England, he lost a limb,
And, generously, it pensioned him.

They had lived on this—with him 'twas gone,
Leaving her friendless—poor—and alone :
She had stitched all night—two farthings won—
" O ! would that this weary life were done ! "

Nor brothers nor sisters e'er had she,
None—ev'n to share her misery—
O ! what pleasure ! starving together !—
Brothers and sisters—she had neither.

She had nor blanket, nor sheet, nor shawl,
To cover her poor shrunk form withal—
Shiv'ring with cold, though her burning skin
Told of the fever that raged within.

Then fell the thoughts—scorchingly keen—
Of what she was now, and once had been,
Hot on her brain—hot, aye burning hot !—
And again she wished that she were not.

Her spirit was broken : strength all gone :
Even for the pittance she had won,

Go she could not, and starve she must—
Of water no drop—of bread no crust !

Words are feeble, they cannot express
How, in the madness of her distress,
She struggled for lack of Bread and Breath—
Starved to death !—Starved to death !

She died that night—when the next day dawned.
In search of the shirts—she had not pawned—
Came one who was callous, yet almost wept
Over her who now her last sleep slept :

Death—always cold—breathed so chilly there !
O'er the corpse—the stool—the old arm-chair—
That his blood turned cold, his teeth, like stones,
Chatter'd together, his very bones

Shook, as if he were palsied and old—
To be out again he'd have given gold,
But his limbs refused, he wished in vain,
And his knees knocked at each other again.

He wept—for, at times, the tears will flow
From the sternest eyes o'er woman's woe
Gazing again on that lifeless clay
Without one friend to bear it away!

.   .

A pauper's burial, half-finished rites—
Grudgingly given—favours, not rights—
Did paupers' souls require their completion,
When, when would they rise to full fruition?

KÖRNER.

OUNG, and brave, and noble-hearted,
Körner died for Fatherland,
With life, and love, and fame he parted —
Boldest of the Jäger band.

O who shall tell the deep devotion
That inspired his daring soul—
Or who its rapturous emotion,
Swaying him with full control !

With laurel wreaths his pen had crowned him,
Now his sword the foe withstood,
And danger ever foremost found him
Striving for his country's good.

Of that career—whose sun in glory
Set so soon, to rise no more,
Save in its song and deathless story—
Who shall read and not deplore ?

As o'er his fate I sadly ponder,
  Wrapt in Sorrow's starless gloom,
Upwelling thoughts unbidden wander
  To the youthful hero's tomb:

Bright groups of seraph-angels hover
  O'er the venerable Oak
Beneath whose shade, life's conflict over,
  Körner feels no foreign yoke:

Hark! their glorious Pæan sounding—
  " FREEDOM IS THY BIRTHRIGHT, MAN!"
The chorus, hark! with joy abounding,
  " IF MEN WOULD BE FREE THEY CAN!"

Methinks I see the poet-soldier
  Standing o'er his honoured grave,
And hear that voice—grown sternly bolder–
  See on high that falchion wave—

" Glorious Pæan! sound thy numbers
  In my sleeping country's ears,
Germany, alas! still slumbers,
  She no song of Freedom hears :—

" How I mourn her worse than slavery !
Kings and priests do lord it still !
But, tyrants, she shall prove her bravery
When awakes UNITED WILL !—

" DAS VOLKSTEHT yet shall rise together,
Shaking off each galling yoke,
Nor rest till every bond they sever,
Till they every chain have broke !—

" UNITED WILL ! with voice like thunder,
Million-tongued, shall strike them dumb,
And pale with fear and wild'ring wonder—
Fleeing as the NATIONS come !

" As I then went shall thousands, gladly,
Bidding life and love farewell :
Fond ones near them grieving sadly,
Looking fears they dare not tell :

" Yes, Germany, Misrule unseating,
Purest Freedom shall attain,
Even now her Eagle's wings are beating
And that Pæan sounds again !—

" Then forward! youths, to death or glory!
  Dear though home and friends may be—
And dying, ye shall live in story,
  Living, see your country free!

" Though Fortune's star be brightly shining,
  Though its cheering influence bind
The soul to life, let no repining
  Quell the ardour of the mind:

" By Heaven, it is a sacred feeling!
  I have felt its holy fire
Through every vein like lightning stealing—
  Till fresh hope did me inspire.

" Though many are too base for living,
  None too good for Freedom die:
Pure Hearts, while your life-off'rings giving,
  Trust that they shall bloom on high:

" No soul can be too great, remember,
  For a great and holy cause;
Fan then to flames each smould'ring ember—
  Forward! turn ye not, nor pause!

" Brave youths ! be rocks on which the nations
  May their hopes of Freedom raise,
Deserve and gain their acclamations,
  And be crowned with deathless bays ;

" What ! tune the lyre to songs of gladness
  Whilst your brethren bravely fight ?
Dance and toy !—delicious madness !—
  Whilst they battle for the right ?

" It may not be ! your God—befriending
  All the loved ones left behind—
His gracious aid for ever lending,
  Will support each fervent mind :

" 'Tis hard—I've known—Life to surrender,
  Life and Friendship—Love and Bliss !—
But all, again ! I'd gladly tender
  To attain an end like this !

          .   .   .   .

He sheathed the Sword no longer gory,
  And rejoined the seraph throng—
Floating with them back to glory,
  Borne upon their wings of song :

Hark! as they rise, the Pæan sounding—

" Freedom is thy birthright, man !

The chorus, hark ! with joy abounding,

" If men would be free, they can !"

THE CAGED LARK.

OOR prison'd Lark! all thy regrets are vain,
    Thou canst not visit the green fields of May:
How'er melodious may be thy strain.
    Here thou art doomed in bondage close to stay.

What! set thee free—to joy with thine own kind
    To revel gladly in the summer air—
To join the throng harmoniously combined
    To banish from each listener gloomy care—?

Ah! it were vain such freedom to bestow!
    They'd deem thee tainted by thy sojourn here.
Would rudely scorn thee—so increase thy woe—
    But here, though prison'd, scorn thou need'st not fear.

Dost note my words, and, noting, think them sage,
   That now thou pourest out thy heart in song?
Art thou content to warble in thy cage—
   Means so that note so clear, so rich, so long ?

Let it be so ! I'll cherish thee, sweet bird !
   As fondly as a mother doth her child,
Will, daily, from the verdant, dewy sward,
   Cut thee a turf whereon the sun hath smiled

Will bring thee stores of field-food, fresh and green,
   Will tempt thy palate with a wondrous choice,
Will strive to gladden thee from morn till e'en,
   And all but satiate thee with little joys :

When comes the sun to smile on youth and age,
   Reviving many a sick and drooping heart,
Outside my window, then, I'll hang thy cage
   There thou shalt sing till his last smiles depart.

What !—louder ! still more joyous than before
   Thou art content, sweet bird, to stay with me !
Then, so am I, to tend thee more and more,
   And spend my leisure hours with books and thee.

OUTSIDERS.

 SAVE us—ere we perish !
 There is no human heart
So foul but it doth cherish
 Some one redeeming part !

Our souls and bodies hunger—
 Will no one give them food ?
Each day we grow but younger,
 And weaker in aught good ;

Yet stronger we, and older,
 In Evil every day—
Experience making bolder,
 And pointing out the way :

We're idle, very idle,
   While others work and win :
The daylight, like a bridle,
   Doth hold us tightly in :

The Summer shines too brightly,
   Its days are long and clear—
In the dreary Winter, nightly,
   We plunder without fear :

But we do not like the star,
   Nor yet the quiet moon,
For our stealthy work they mar
   And always rise too soon—

Rise soon, and never weary,
   But shine through all the night,
And aye seem coming near ye
   With their eyes so sharp and bright.

To us those streets are lonely
   Whose lights seem bright as day—
The hated Workhouse only
   Awaits us round the way—

Outsiders.

Or the prison—so what wonder
  If for money or for bread
We risk an open plunder,
  Even caught, we're hous'd and fed ?

Like rats—just human vermin—
  We, skulking, steal for food :
O ye of wigs and ermine !
  Can ye not do us good ?

O ! is there nothing for us
  But law's strong, vengeful grip ?
Is there really nothing for us
  But hulk, or cage, or whip ?

O save us ! ere we perish !
  There is no human heart
So foul but it doth cherish
  Some one redeeming part !

THE POET'S MISSION.

HIS golden truth must be inwove
    With what the Poet teacheth—
GOD'S LOVE surviveth life and time,
    And all decay out-reacheth.

Imagination's noblest flight,
    And most sublime emotion,
Have birth within the sacred pale
    Of man's sincere devotion.

Religion is no puzzling scheme
    Of doctrines weirdly mystic—
Existeth not in pomp and show,
    Emblazon'd and artistic—

Divinely plain, thus runs its creed—
  On God be all-depending,
Do as thou would'st be done unto,
  And leave to Him the ending.

Those workers must needs earnest be
  Who seek the mind's dominion—
Truthful as earnest, if they mean
  To live in good opinion.

The Beautiful and True, combined,
  Define the Bard's vocation,
And when his wing'd words touch the world
  How great the world's ovation !

To teach Goodwill and Brotherhood,
  The love of all that liveth—
The Law of Kindness, and the joys
  That visit those who giveth :

Of candour, honesty, and truth,
  To shew the common duty—
Of the forgiving heart to paint
  The holiness and beauty :

To dwell on Love's enduring power—
    On Passion's brief duration—
To laud those pure and lofty lives
    That render great a nation :

To trace His hand in ev'ry flower—
    The meanest never scorning—
In ev'ry glory-flashing star
    The crown of night adorning : —

Such teachings flow like living streams
    From Poesie's true fountain,
And cheer the trav'ller while he scales
    The lofty Epic mountain :

And many a sweetly simple Lay
    The heart of man enshrineth—
To yield a never ending joy,
    To speak when none divineth.

The Sower may not live to reap
    Reward for what he soweth,
Yet still have faith that, in the end,
    Good seed to fruitage groweth :

The Poet's Work outlives his Life—
His truths outlive decrying,
And flourish green amidst decay
And Men and Nations dying !

Outlines in Verse.

THE JEW OF SIDON.

IN Sidon, in the olden time,
  There dwelt one Abel Maiht,
A man just in his manhood's prime,
  Of honourable state.

Ten years had Abel wedded been
  To Jessica Nursyee,
But child of his he ne'er had seen,
  And sorely grievéd he.

One day sat Abel all alone
  Within a sweet alcove,
O'er his broad lands the bright sun shone
  And warmed them with its love.

" And must these fair domains descend
    To one, no son of mine—
Lands, gold, and all, to but a friend—
    Not ev'n of mine own line—? "

So mourned aloud sad Abel Maiht—
    His head upon his breast—
Much he bewailed his childless state,
    And much was he depressed ;

When, suddenly, his downcast eye
    Flashed with some happy thought—
He snapp'd his fingers and leapt high,
    With frantic joy o'erwrought—

" I have it now ! I have it now ! "
    The Israelite exclaimed,
" Dissolved shall be my marriage vow,
    I'll seek some Rabbi famed."

First, and straightway, he sought his wife,
    And gently to her broke
His wish to cast off, without strife,
    His present wedded yoke :

She wept, she sobb'd—hot tears fell fast—
She wept and sobb'd in vain—
" Nay, wife." said he, " this need not last,
We must. and shall be twain ! "

That day to Rabbi Simon he
His downcast partner led.
And skilfully, and earnestly,
For a divorce he pled:

Stood Jessica, as statue pale,
Woe-stricken—crushed at heart—
Yet wept no tear, let forth no wail,
But felt that they must part.

" 'Tis true, indeed," the Rabbi said,
" Thou a divorce canst claim,
But think how long thou hast been wed
To this good worthy dame."

Vain were his words, and vain her woe,
The Jew would have his way ;
Which seeing, Simon said, " be't so,
But list to me, I pray—

" When you were wedded, to your friends
    A sumptuous feast you gave,
So do you now, such small amends
    For her great loss I crave :

" Your parting, like your union, thus
    Shall duly honoured be,
And one so truly virtuous
    All this deserves of thee :

" That done, return to me and I
    Will grant what you desire—
I'd have ye part all pleasantly,
    And not in hate and ire,"

They both agreed, and homeward hied
    The banquet to prepare,
And to invite—next eventide—
    Their friends the feast to share.

The cheer was plentiful as good,
    Of guests there were not few,
And all had donned their happiest mood—
    All sadness to eschew.

Thus all was well, what must be, must,
    Each wisely had bethought,
So held their faces from the dust
    And set old Care at nought.

Soon as the wine did merr'ly flow,
    Rich Abel's heart grew warm,
And very tenderly to glow
    Beneath its potent charm :

" Dear wife—dear Jessica," said he,
    " To show we kindly part,
I pray thou wilt take hence with thee
    What most delights thy heart—

" My house's richest treasure take—
    Whate'er it be, 'tis thine—
Preserve it for thy Abel's sake—
    His heart shall aye be thine."

The sparkling cup went round and round,
    Both host and guests drank free,
And soon lay stretched upon the ground
    Asleep—right heavilie !

Before the potent wine began
  To muddle Abel's brain,
Poor Jessica conceived a plan
  Her husband to retain :

Thought she, I'll keep him to his word
  When sound asleep he lies,
The house no treasure can afford
  Like Abel in my eyes.

The Jew was on a litter laid,
  And to her father's borne,
There placed upon the daintiest bed—
  Nor woke he till the morn :

But such a waking !—how he stared
  And started with surprise !
Like tiger trapped, around he glared
  With wild and wond'ring eyes :

" Where—where am I ?" he cried, at last,
  " How—wherefore am I here ?—
What place is this ?—Are my dreams past ?-–
  No ! still I dream, I fear :"

"No dream," cried Jessica, "no dream
  (She watched him all the night);
Be calm, nor so bewilder'd seem,
  This house is Zadoc's hight:"

"And wherefore I in Zadoc's?—say!"
  "My lord, be not surprised,
Last night thou bad'st me take away
  Aught from thy house I prized—

"Now Earth holds nothing that to me
  Is dearer than thyself,
Thy gold and jewels without thee
  Are filthy dross and pelf—

"Thou art the wealth which I would hoard,
  Without thee, life were death—
Cast me not from thee, my good lord,
  Think on my love!—my faith!"

She ceased—he clasped her to his heart—
  "My wife! my wife!" he cried,
"How could I think from thee to part?
  Live ever by my side!"

Home they returned, nor e'er again
  Was parting spoke of there,
And when had passed years—other ten—
  She blest him with an heir !

AUTUMN LEAVES.

UTUMN leaves! why should ye perish,
    Lying cold and low?
Are there no friendly hands to cherish,
    And avert such woe?

        Lying cold and low,
            Damp and cold and low—
        Are there no friendly hands to cherish,
            And avert such woe?

When Summer days were warmly shining
    Ye lent kindly shade,
And many a pleasant hour of shelter
    In this forest glade—

Lying cold and low,
　　Damp and cold aud low—
Are there no friendly hands to cherish,
　　And avert such woe ?

Autumn leaves ! why should ye wither,
　　Wither and decay—
Russet, crimson, and rich golden,
　　Fading all away ?

　　Lying cold and low,
　　　　Damp and cold and low—
　　Are there no friendly hands to cherish,
　　　　And avert such woe ?

　.　　　.　　　.　　　.　　　.

" All of earth must fade and perish,
　　We but go before,
And Man with all he loves to cherish
　　Falleth evermore—

　　Lying cold and low,
　　　　Damp and cold and low,—
　　Are there no friendly hands to cherish,
　　　　And avert his woe ? "

OVER THE SEA.

I.

AND must we fly our country
   For earth's remotest shores ?
Must we, like outcast children,
   Be driven from her doors ?
What have we done to merit
   All but the foul disgrace
Of that convicted felon—
   Crime written on his face ?

II.

Have we not toiled from childhood,
   From early morn till e'en ?
Have we not racked our bodies,
   While crush'd our souls have been ?

L

We've neither begg'd nor idled—
  Are honest, hand and heart—
Count every man a brother,
  And with the weak take part.

III.

In working we take pleasure,
  Each of his art is proud,
And would exert the talents
  With which he is endowed :
We wish but for employment—
  We wish and ask in vain—
Our marts are overflowing—
  The answer is too plain :

IV.

We are not discontented,
  The spirit of our laws—
Though needing reformation—
  Calls forth our hearts' applause :
We're freemen, all, and know it,
  Nor do we disagree
With those who say no people
  Are half so great or free—

V.

But privileges never
  Will feed or clothe a man,
We must have food and wages—
  Find them where best we can :
Thousands have gone before us
  Where we are going now,
And millions yet will follow
  To sow and Speed the Plough—

VI.

Unless they till our home-wastes—
  Enrich our native soil—
Home-acres fit for culture
  Await the sons of toil—
Hill-sides, and moors, and valleys,
  Need but the human hand
To render them as fertile
  As our adopted land :

VII.

No need of Emigration,
  Here's room enough for all
Were but the land delivered
  From that vile feudal thrall—

Why lags emancipation ?
  The many, not the few,
Are destined to possess it
  And reap thence Labour's due.

VIII.

Strong in this hope we leave thee.
  Our own dear native land.
Warm hearts for us are weeping
  Upon thy rocky strand—
And thou and they for ever
  Shall in our memories dwell
We can but leave our blessing—
  Farewell ! dear land, farewell !

FAREWELL TO THE HEATHER!

AREWELL to the heather!
 Farewell to the North,
From the home of our fathers
 The lairds drive us forth ;
Now the sheep and red deer
 Are better than men,
And there's woe on the hill-side
 And eke in the glen.

Farewell to the heather !
 We'll tread it no more—
Our last hope on earth
 Is Columbia's shore ;
Ere the sun sink to rest
 We shall sail o'er the sea—
A new home to seek
 In a far countrie.

Farewell to the heather !—
  The heather's on fire—
The flames from our shielings
  Rise higher and higher !
May his Grace, the Lord Duke,
  Never feel as we feel—
While we turn our last look
  On the land of the leal!

Farewell to the heather !
  Come prairie and wood,
Our strong arms we bring you,
  And strong hearts and good—
If soldiers are wanted,
  Let laurels of fame
Be gather'd by shepherds
  And keepers of game.

" SHAKSPEARE."

HAT glorious victories are here enshrined
    In deathless trophies of immortal Mind !
What proud exemption from the common doom
Are lives that need no costly, storied tomb !
How rich the spoils from Death's cold clutches wrung—
How vast the fame that lives on ev'ry tongue !

Such fame is thine, thou first of human kind
By whom the soul's deep myst'ries were defined :
Thou held'st the mirror up to nature's view
And proved the false by setting forth the true :
Dissecting motives of the hidden will
With touch precise and anatomic skill,
Unlocking ev'ry chamber of the heart
That laughs—or weeps, at bidding of thy Art.

Sun of thy system ! whose effulgent rays

Dispel the filmy clouds of mental haze,
Clearing the lab'rinths of Life's devious way
Till darkness seems transparent as the day—
Still unapproached throughout the World of Mind,
All Coming Time shall fail thy like to find !

MASTER LOVE.

OVE'S a naughty, changeful boy—
Now he's forward, now he's coy—
Now he romps in glad excess—
Now he sighs in deep distress—
     Heigh-ho, the fellow !

Love like a chameleon seems
Formed of ever-changing whims:
Now he blushes, now grows pale—
Now he'll flatter, now he'll rail—
     Heigh-ho, the fellow !

Love's an artful little thing—
Sly the glances he can fling—
Now brings pleasures, now brings pains,
Now implores and now disdains—
     Heigh-ho, the fellow !

Would that Love had ne'er been born
And our hearts left quite forlorn !—
Better so than thus to be
Tossed on an inconstant sea—
   Heigh-ho, the fellow !

MY MOTHER.

SHE sleeps, her thin pale cheek upon her hand—
    Her face, towards the light, receives the dawn
That streameth gently o'er the placid brow,
The closéd eyelids, and soft moulded lips
So pleasingly disposed into a smile :
Repose so sweet, so peaceful and profound,
Hath been estranged from her for many a year—
Some say that Age a second Childhood knows,
Enjoying oft its pleasant balmy sleep,
How welcome such must be to her—at last !

She many long and weary vigils kept—
Sustained by a brave spirit, and a hope
That never faileth in the faith inspired,

And sleeps she now so calmly, and so long?
Alas! it is a sleep that ne'er shall know
Disturbance more—the last, long sleep of all!
And yet I read no closing conflict here,
The soul, when summon'd from its shattered shrine,
Withdrew so peacefully that dreaded Death
Wears but the semblance of an earthly sleep.

GOOD WALTER.

OBIT. CHRISTMASTIDE, MDCCCLXX.

In losing his own life my brother did save two others, therefore he did not die
in vain.—A. F. WALTER.

EROES have been who did not yield
To death upon a battle field—
So gave he up a noble life
Unsullied by the rage of strife.

He loseth not his life in vain
Whose loss to others counteth gain,
And o'er Good Walter's early tomb
The amaranths of fame shall bloom.

Who would not envy death like this?
Sure passport to eternal bliss—
To welcome from the man above
Who sacrificed his Life for Love:

Let grateful hearts, then, open wide
As falls each holy Christmas-tide—
Let rescued lives teach men anew,
Do as Ye would Be Done Unto!

OVER THE MOUNTAINS.

OVER the mountains,
  Or over the sea,
Roam, let us roam,
Bold, fearless, and free—
We shall ne'er have a care,
We shall ne'er give a sigh,
With thoughts aye unclouded
And hearts beating high.

The home of the brave
Is where liberty reigns,
On huge towering mountains
Or ocean's vast plains—
Though storms whistle o'er us
We'll heed not the blast,
But Rovers, bold Rovers,
Remain to the last.

We'll rise with the lark,
With the sun sink to rest,
And dark sorrow banish
Away from each breast :
With a blue sky above
And a fair earth beneath,
We'll scale the steep mountain
Or tread the lone heath.

O Freedom, blest Freedom !
How bright are the rays
That dart from thy sunbeams
And scatter the haze—
That enrich the proud waves
As they dash on the strand—
On the bold rocky shores
Of our Native Land !

IDOLS.

 WOULD that I were a child again
    And my sole delight a toy—
Such never could look or speak unkind,
    But for ever yield me joy !

The hopes of the world are false and vain,
    Its hearts are hollow and cold,
And the cruel blight of some cherisht love
    A story too often told.

The Idols we raise are swept away
    By old Time's resistless flow,
While the broken heart of Bereavement sinks
    To the deepest depths of woe.

And rest there is none for the weary life
Except where the willows wave—
No certain peace, no calm repose,
But low in the silent grave.

FAR, FAR AWAY!

THE joys of home and youth depart
　　As time rolls swiftly on,
And long ere age hath chilled the heart
　　Its brightest hopes have flown ;
But most we mourn the absent friends
　　Whose mem'ries ne'er decay—
Whose distant home enchantment lends—
　　　　　　Far, far away.

'Tis hard to think we may not meet
　　And be as we have been,
While yet our warm life-pulses beat
　　In recollection keen :
Though oft kind greetings come and go,
　　And each for each doth pray,
We still must wish they were not so
　　　　　　Far, far away.

The winds that float across the deep
    And kiss the crested waves
Seem wailing o'er the dead that sleep
    Far down in ocean's caves,
Yet oft, when wand'ring o'er the sands,
    Methinks I've heard them say—
" Remember friends in distant lands
            Far, far away."

O could we hear them speak again !
    And clasp their hands once more,
And dear-united friends remain—
    As we have been before !
That such a joy may crown our lot
    Most fervently we'll pray,
Though absent they are not forgot—
            Far, far away !

A WEDDING GIFT.

LL that I have this day is thine,
   A heart whose faith has never falter'd.
A love that knew no other shrine
   And through all changes lives unalter'd.
Had I thousand hearts to give
   Thine all their love and faith should be,
Had I a thousand years to live
   I'd gladly spend them all with thee.

There's not a joy in all the world
   Like that of Love beyond deceiving,
Though bolt on bolt be at it hurled
   The heart will triumph—when believing.

This day my joy hath sov'reign sway—
A joy which but with thee I know,
The rapture of a first, fond love
Which, wedded, makes a heaven below!

HOME REVISITED.

HERISHT scenes of my youth, I revisit you now
With the footsteps of years on my time-trodden
    brow—
With the shadows of care where the smiles of hope shone,
Ere the dreamings of youth had all faded and gone.

Yet my heart seems as young in the bliss it now feels
As it was when in boyhood I clamber'd these hills.
Nay, I know not if ever I felt when a boy
Such vivid sensations of rapturous joy.

Though the years have wrought changes on you, as on me,
Still unalter'd remains this fair arm of the sea,
This world-renown'd frith, my own beautiful Clyde !
O'er whose breast I was wont in my shallop to glide :

When I launch'd my frail bark on its shining expanse
How gaily, how proudly, o'er it was our dance!
Nor sought we the shore till the sun's dying ray
Had fled from the gaze of the long summer day.

There, too, still unchanged, rise the old giant hills
Interlaced as of yore by their rock-bedded rills,
Heather-clad as they were in the centuries fled
When the Clans of the Shires for their liberty bled.

Should some boasting invaders e'er visit these shores
They may not be met with the ancient claymores,
But the sharp, deadly ring of our rifles shall tell
That the Sons of the Gael love their liberty well!

LOVE'S EDEN.

 NEVER thought this world could be
The Eden that it is to me,
Nor ever in my vision'd dreams,
My aspirations or their themes,
Had pictured bliss so truly great
A portion of our mortal state.
Give Fashion's slaves their bright display,
Give Monarchs empires, thrones, and sway,
I only ask that of thy heart
Mine shall remain a living part.
No outward signs need Love bestow
To cause affection's streams to flow—
There is a strange mysterious bond
Our narrow knowledge far beyond
That heart with heart, and mind with mind,
In closest union blend and bind :

From thee, a kindly word can raise
My spirit in its darkest days—
From thee, a warm, impassion'd kiss
Transports me to a realm of bliss !
Thy truth and love endeareth life,
Soothes all its care, quells all its strife,
And more thy faithfulness to me
Than all the wealth of land or sea.
Come, dearest, nestle on my breast !
Be it thy ever-welcome rest—
And in thy heart I'll make my home
Withouten wish beyond to roam :
Believe me, where such love hath birth
There is much more of heaven than earth—
And this believe, all things above,
LOVE springs from Heaven, and Heaven is Love !

THE INNER WORLD.

HOUGH rays of memory gild the past
  And former joys renew,
Their bright enchantments never last
  But swiftly fade from view.

Thus through the brain will lov'd ones pass
  Their vacant chairs to fill—
Yet ere our gaze is fixt, alas !
  We find them empty still !

Unknown to us, from Spirit land,
  Our dear ones may return
And all the feelings understand
  Of hearts that sigh and yearn—

May know when faithful mourners bring
    Their faces back once more,
Or when their voices seem to ring
    In gladness as of yore.

Have such the power to visit us—
    In spirit though it be—
In sorrow and in happiness?
    In heaviness and glee?

    .   .   .

Life is—through Life—a myst'ry seal'd,
    The Truth but glimmers through,
But with the Change shall be reveal'd
    The Old blent with the New.

MY LOVE.

 WOULD like my love to be trusting,
   As trusting as if she were blind,
I would wish her to lean on me wholly,
   With never a doubt on her mind.

With all that pertains to the struggles—
   The battles and bargains of life—
It is fit that a man should be laden,
   But keep woman out of the strife.

Her world is that home where affection
   Is foster'd and nurtur'd and spread,
And the woman that makes it most happy
   Works more with her heart than her head.

I would like my love to be cultur'd—
Not over, yet highly, refined—
Leading me with her beautiful instinct,
And not by the strength of her mind.

CLOUDS.

ET us hope for a to-morrow
When the clouds will flee away—
And so from the future borrow
Gleams of comfort for to-day.

When we know the sun is shining
Just behind the filmy haze,
Well we know its golden lining
Will appear in coming days.

We have but to wait and reason
That what is is for the best,
And at last will come our season
Of enduring joy and rest.

Let us hope for that to-morrow
Which contentment only brings
And in passing Clouds of Sorrow
See the Hands that are the King's.

WAR AND CONQUEST.

RITE brutish war and conquest down
   Ye men of intellectual might—
On wrongs in Earth's high places frown,
   And flood dark Error's caves with light !

For Mercy, as for Justice, plead,
   Let War be intellectual strife—
While we have Reason where the need
   To sacrifice dear human life ?

The God-made, God-like, creature, Man,
   No longer must, by King or Law,
Be set up in the battle-van
   And shot at like a targe of straw.

If Kings and Emperors will fight
    With other weapons than the Pen,
Let them each other singly smite
    And cease to slaughter hosts of men.

King-craft and State-craft, crying, " more,"
    Have curst us with a second flood—
Their blind, unholy lust of power
    Re-deluging the Earth with blood.

Uncounted, countless millions thus
    Have paved the paths which now we tread -
Their very dust re-lives in us—
    We are but offsprings of the dead.

O would that now were shadow'd forth
    The joys of that long promised time
When all the Nations of the Earth
    Shall dwell unstained by blood or crime !

When spears shall into pruning hooks,
    And swords to willing ploughshares turn
When War shall only live in books,
    Or on the mould'ring trophied urn !

UNDER THE CLOUD.

A LAY OF THE LANCASHIRE FAMINE.

LIFE of my bosom ! children of mine !
Do not despair though our fortunes decline—
The clouds may be heavy, the storms may be near,
But the heart that is trusting has conquer'd its fear.

Home may be humble, but still it is home,
A region of peace whence we seek not to roam,
A shrine of delight that the world never knows,
A haven of blissful and welcome repose.

Wife of my bosom ! there once was a time
When our hopes of the future were truly sublime,
When Want held no place in our visions of bliss—
When we never contemplated sorrow like this.

Wife of my bosom! I see through the clouds
Faint gleams of a joy which the present but shrouds.
And as with the sun when withheld from our sight.
The warmth of its influence heralds the light.

Despair not, my lov'd ones, the Night will depart,
And the bright rays of Morning re-gladden each heart -
United in love let us brave out the blast
And Faith. o'er Misfortune, shall triumph at last!

CRYSTALLYNE.

TAKE away the passion-cup !
   I may not taste the sparkling wine,
Though told that in the quaffing up
   There dwells an ecstacy divine.

I will not drown ennobling thought,
   Or drive the reason from my brain,
The pleasure is too dearly bought
   That bringeth after-grief and pain.

Kind Nature doth on us bestow
   A gift more precious than the Vine,
And freely from her fountains flow
   The glorious streams of Crystallyne

Temptation bubbles o'er the Cup,
But I'll resist the fatal bliss,
Too well I know the quaffing up
Would only prove a Judas-kiss !

HARVEST HYMN.

1870.

 God! for this bountiful harvest
Let the souls of Thy people be joyful.
Let their hearts overflow with thanksgiving—
Let their lips utter praises triumphant!

As we mow down the full-ripen'd treasures
May we think of their Great Creator,
As we bind up the great golden sheaves
May we inwardly thank Thee. O Father!

We still own the blessings of peace
To crown the full comforts of plenty,
While the demons of carnage and death
Are slaying our fellows by thousands.

Thine Arm hath been so long around us,
And thy Right Arm hath so long provided,
That we, in the pride of our hearts,
Now deem ourselves heirs of security.

We suppose ourselves marked out and chosen
As those to whom all earthly blessings
Shall for ever flow forth in abundance —
From the depths of a limitless ocean.

O God ! 'midst this bountiful harvest,
May the pride of our hearts be unharden'd :
We bend ourselves lowly before Thee—
Our Shield and our only Sustainer !

LET HOPE BE EVER YOUNG.

———

THE faery dreams of former years
  Have faded quite away,
And in their place there but appears
  Some token of decay.

Where now the bounding gush of joy
  From youth's bright fount that sprung?
Where now the bliss without alloy
  When Hope and I were young?

The fount is dry, the gush is o'er,
  No trace of beauty seen,
And I, bereaved for evermore,
  But grieve for what has been.

Away! away! each gloomy thought
  Behind me shall be flung –
While life holds on 'tis promise-fraught—
  Let Hope be ever young!

BONNIE INVERMAY.

'VE roamed afar where'er the star
    Of Fortune guided me,
But till this day, sweet Invermay,
    I've ne'er forgotten thee.
Time rolls along while sigh and song
    In swift succession flow,
For smiles and tears, and hopes and fears,
    Are all of life we know :
        Yet dear to me shall ever be
        The joy of life's young day,
        And still shall I, till mem'ry die,
        Love Bonnie Invermay !

I love the glens, the rocky glens,
    Of our romantic land,
I love her hills, her heath'ry hills,
    And mountains sternly grand !

O for the days, the happy days,
  When Hope's bright cup ran o'er!
But all in vain I sigh again—
  They'll gladden me no more :
    Yet dear to me shall ever be
      The joy of life's young day,
    And still shall I, till mem'ry die,
      Love Bonnie Invermay!

I love the streams, the bounding streams,
  That Echo loves to greet,
That dance and play, and fall in spray,
  Like diamonds at our feet ;
And should Fate's star lead me afar—
  Or strew my path with care,
Till sorrows grow, and age's snow
  Hath whiten'd every hair—
    Still dear to me shall ever be
      The joy of life's young day,
    And still shall I, till mem'ry die,
      Love Bonnie Invermay.

THE SPIRIT-GOAL.

E may not mourn the spirit's flight
From darkness to unclouded light !
We cannot wish that it had stayed—
Of earth-blights—earth-damps—sore afraid :
And yet, we're human—life-love, how human !
Earthy, how earthy !—strong man, frail woman :
For ever clinging to this narrow sphere
And mocking higher hopes we grovel here.

We have a hope—a blesséd hope !
With sin and death 'tis fit to cope
When link'd with faith—O fearless faith !
That in the unfathom'd sea of Death
Leaps boldly from the giant rock of Time—
Which it took long and weary years to climb—

Floating away   away to eternity--
Breathing the blissful air of infinity !

Her's was that hope, and her's that faith
Which lulls the stormy waves of death—
O ! how she wished to be away—
Away from night to lasting day !
From its love and hate   its joy and sorrow:
Now she knows no night—fears no to-morrow :
Glory eternal !—changeless—for ever—
Is the joy of believers—fading never !

Cease to repine—she is happier far
Than ye e'er could have made her— than ye are :
Wherefore be downcast ?—strive to be with her
When ye leave this pilgrim-world for ever :
Grace is abounding !—Heaven without limit !
Struggle on !--still on !—till ye are in it !

WATERLOO.

THE hero of a hundred fights
   All honour to his name!
The champion of our dearest rights
   Enshrine in deathless fame!
And most of all his victories—
   So signal and so true—
Let us remember with delight
   The one at Waterloo!

Embroil'd perhaps we yet had been
   With Gallia as a foe
Had Wellington with iron arm
   Not laid the spoiler low:

From Elba flushed with hope he came
  To threaten us anew,
But, crushed at last, his prowess died
  On famous Waterloo !

Of glory full, and full of years,
  The hero passed away—
The nation wept a sea of tears-
  The world bewailed the day !
And though we trust that ne'er again
  We'll have such work to do,
Let Britons never once forget
  The Duke and Waterloo !

DECEIT.

LAS ! that Deceit should e'er dwell
  'Neath a smile so angelic as thine ;
That around thy sweet tongue—all unseen—
Such a venomous reptile should twine !

Thy lips are as soft still, and bright,
  As they were when I loved thee so well.
Yet, loathing, I turn me away,
  For within lurks a spirit of hell !

I trust that the power of thine eyes
  May ne'er draw me towards thee again,
The poison which thine would impart
  My own lips might incline to retain.

It cost me a pang to refrain
  From the fruit I had relished so long,
Yet, strengthen'd, I conquer'd myself,
  And I tender my thanks in my song.

CHILDHOOD.

PRETTY little fairy creature!
  Guileless glee in every feature :
Free from art's deceits and wiles,
Full of joyous hopes and smiles.

Those sweet eyes, so brightly shining,
Tell thou know'st not of repining :
They only speak of joy—below
That forehead pure and white as snow.

Thy cheeks must love the fond caresses
Of those playful golden tresses :
Mimic sunbeams kissing roses
Ere their too brief summer closes!

O the happy round of childhood !
Sunny mead and shady wildwood—
Flowery glens and faëry streams :
Soothing songs and shining dreams !

FREE FATHERLAND.

WAKE ! arise ! Great German Land !
Shake off for aye the iron-hand—
Shake off the galling yoke of caste
And hail fair Freedom's dawn at last—
Germania must and shall be free !
From hill to vale, from lake to sea !

Thy blood has flown in torrents forth
The life-blood of the mighty North
And Liberty is fitting crown
For deeds of deadly-bought renown
Germania must and shall be free !
From hill to vale, from lake to sea !

Your Kaiser-King may never hear
The chorus pealing deep and clear,
But sound it shall with potent voice
The list'ning nations to rejoice—
    Thus shall it ring—BE EVER FREE !
    FROM HILL TO VALE, FROM LAKE TO SEA !

PROSE OR POESIE ?

AN EPISTLE TO JAMES BALLANTINE, EDINBURGH.

HAT wordy fallow, Tam Carlyle,
    In unctuous, mentorian style.
The bardic callin' daurs revile,
          And skys his prose.

Noo, I hae tried, and that in vain,
An' ettled ower an' ower again,
To howk up facts, doonricht and plain,
          Frae oot his beuks.

An' I hae cam to this conclusion—
That he's the King o' Phraseconfusion,
An' Laird o' Muckleworddelusion—
          An' ither ilks.

I wadna gie thae screeds o' rhyme
That Burns has handed doon to time
For a' the volumes o' sublime
   By Tammas writ.

I wadna gie your " Drap o' Dew,"
Or " Castles in the Air," sae true,
Wi' mony mair I hae in view,
   For miles o' prose.

Mair fu' o' feelin' than o' art,
The trenchant lyric, like a dart,
Strikes to the universal heart,
   For evermair.

Faur ower the wide Atlantic's wave,
Whaur howlin' tempests roar and rave,
Our Scottish Sangs hae fand nae grave,
   But daithless fame !

Sae, brither James, our eldest bardie,
Let na yer Muse be shy or tardy,
It seems a lang time since we heard ye
   Pipin' her reed.

Dinna mistak' this frien'ly letter,
I ken your wee bit lassie better
Than think that Tammas could her fetter -
        Or steek thy mou'.

While tons on tons o' leaden prose
Sink to a nameless, dark repose,
The cheery sang but wider throws
        Its gowden ray!

"A man's a man for a' that," still
The worl's enraptured ear doth fill,
An' reapeth hairvests o' gudewill
        Frae pole to pole.

.   .   .

I jist hae heard sweet "Huntingtower"
Sang wi a wondrous witchin power—
An' noo, ance mair, she's dirlin't ower,
        Wi' blythsome birr!

THE END.

THIRD EDITION.

By the same Author, preparing for Publication,

IN CROWN 8VO,

THE DAWN OF LOVE.

And other Poems.

OPINIONS OF THE PRESS, ETC.

" This gentleman can write poetry really worth the reading. There is a sea-like freshness in many of his pieces, and a pathos and strength of feeling in others, which bespeak him of the class of men whose world within gives ready and healthy response to the world without."—*British Quarterly Review*.

" The eventful years which have passed over the head of society since Mr. Rae-Brown first published have not been thrown away on the poet. Maturity of judgment and facility of composition are manifested in the original pieces here presented, which are numerous. There is an exceeding variety of brief, vigorous, brilliant bursts on subjects of the passing hour."—*British Banner*.

" The dedication of your poems confers on me an unmerited distinction. I shall owe it to your hearty friendship. I have always welcomed your writings, because of the warm human sympathies they evince—the freshness of imagery they display, and the purity of the style in which the ideas are clothed. Continue to avoid the spasmodic and obscure. Unaffected simplicity is power.—*Thomas de Quincey*.

" They exhibit much vigour of thought and elegance of fancy."—*Morning Post*.

" The lays and lyrics forming this volume exhibit an amount of poetic ability, and a command of language, which will tend to give them a welcome at the hands of a public to whom poetic excellence, in a new writer, appears only as an occasional quality."—*Weekly Dispatch*.

" The author is never moody. He does not trill his lyre in strains of mere sentiment. Had we room, however, to repeat his ' Faitherless Laddie,' that piece would show that, in a strain that would have done honour to Burns, he can be indeed pathetic."—*Christian Times*.

" Mr. Rae-Brown aims at the beautiful, and admirably he succeeds. His great school is Nature, and his effusions are full of a feeling both grateful and true. He is ever fresh, lively, full of warmth and happiness.—The verses we have just quoted display a noble development of the finer feelings or sympathies, and prove that Nature makes the poet."—*Ladies' Newspaper*.

" An elegant volume. The stanzas exhibit considerable elegance of diction and great delicacy of sentiment, and their peculiar charm of music and sweetness of thought will gain them much favour."—*Leader*.

" The volume we have named is by a contributor of ours, and our readers have, therefore, a very general knowledge of its merits. On that account we do not quote largely, but the following extracts will show that the style is powerful and diversified."—*Tait's Magazine*.

" Another Scottish writer comes in aid of the proof, that the land of Burns continues to be the land of song. The ' Widow's Daughter ' is one of the most tender and touching descriptions; philanthropic as well as patriotic feelings are breathed throughout. ' Lines to a Child Asleep' open with much simple beauty.' *Literary Gazette*.

" He belongs to a school of ' prophets' who are deserving of all encouragement, especially as among them we do not despair of hearing some high Habakkuk voice swelling up into a loftier and louder strain. *Hogg's Instructor*.

" I have been reading your poems with much pleasure, and shall begin again from the first page, for already I am aware how well and pleasantly my time will be employed." *Walter Savage Landor*.

Opinions of the Press, etc.

"Their freshness of thought and simplicity of style arrest the attention, while they elevate the mind of the reader. There is truthfulness, warm and genial as summer sunshine, dwelling about and reposing among those 'Lays and Lyrics.'" *Critic.*

"The author has given us one or two sweet little pictures which are unquestionably touched with the magic light that no one but a true poet ever describes on sea or land. The sonnets exhibit, besides, a beautiful serious faith." *Glasgow Daily Mail.*

"Mr. Rae-Brown is a bard of considerable standing and fame. He has contributed a variety of productions to the Dublin University and other magazines and periodicals. Sweetness and taste uniformly pervade his verse, while a profuse outpouring of gentle fancies renders them exceedingly attractive.—*Glasgow Citizen.*

"Has the heart and mind of a poet." *Glasgow Examiner.*

"Poetry of a genuine description, the free and spontaneous outpouring of that living spirit, which, to him by whom it is possessed, and to him on whom it lavishes its treasures, is 'a joy for ever.' We are free to acknowledge the claims of Mr. Rae-Brown to be admitted a member of that sacred brotherhood whose office it is to awaken and enlighten men by their inspiration of song. In these 'Lays and Lyrics' he contributes his mite towards the accomplishment of the great end, the education of the beautiful in art and nature. 'Lays and Lyrics' are the effusions of a graceful fancy and a feeling heart. They appeal to the sympathies, to all that is truest and worthiest in human nature; and they do not appeal in vain." *Glasgow Constitutional.*

"We hold it to be specially the mission of the poet in the present day to give a voice of thunder to 'the still sad music of humanity'—to do battle with crushing social wrong to brighten the dark horizon of despair with the sunshine of the beautiful, the hopeful, and the true—to 'give songs in the night' to the weary and 'o'er-laboured'—to flash the light of truth into the festering core of every system of error and oppression; to awaken the dead soul to such a sense of its high destiny as will make it feel, amid all the conventualities of life, amid all that is adventitious and accidental, that 'a man's a man for a' that.' Mr. Rae-Brown succeeds best in those lyrics that are directed towards this end, and we rejoice that he has concentrated his talent of song to the cause of human progress."—*Commonwealth.*

"Good poetry in the present day is so rare a production that we rejoice to bring this volume before our readers. It gives elegant utterance to some of the finest feelings of the human heart, and to a very considerable amount of sagacious wisdom, which proves the author to be a poet, not in the sense of a man who makes a jingle of words, but in the sense of a man who thinks deeply."—*Rock.*

"Full of warm human sympathies, and with a quick eye for the picturesque and beautiful, he finds ample scope for his muse among the joys and sorrows which chequer ordinary life, and the 'shows and forms' of nature which diversify the surface of our fair globe. In the crowded city, he beholds much that is anything but beautiful. The 'still, sad music of humanity' touches his soul, and he appeals on behalf of the victims of neglect and vice. Mr. Rae-Brown, albeit a poet, is no idle dreamer, but a thoroughly practical philanthropist of the school of Thomas Hood, Charles Mackay, and Walter Savage Landor." *Paisley Journal.*

"The 'Dawn of Love' is a charming poem, pure in sentiment, and pious in purpose."—*Liverpool Courier.*

"A touching, simple tale, which at times rises with sweet majesty The reader should be a better man after its perusal than before."—*Tunbridge Wells Gazette.*

"Reflects credit on the head and heart of the author—whether viewed as a poem of great merit and beauty, as a valuable contribution to healthy poetic literature, as a testimony to the vital power of Christianity, or as a successful exposition of the nature, effect, and issue of truly virtuous love."—*Northern Ensign.*

"Beautiful sonnets; expressing in language, elegant and musical, much delicacy of sentiment, and charming sweetness of thought: peculiarities which will recommend them to every lover of true poetry." *Falkirk Herald.*